About the Author

Angel Martinez is the erotic fiction pen name of a writer of several genres. Her experiences as a soldier, a nurse, a banker, and an underpaid corporate drone give her a broad view of the world and a deep appreciation for the astounding variety of people on this small planet.

She currently lives part time in the hectic sprawl of northern Delaware and full time inside her head. She has one husband of over twenty years, one son, two cats, a love of all things beautiful and a terrible addiction to the consumption of both knowledge and chocolate.

Website:
http://www.freewebs.com/angelwrites

Facebook:
https://www.facebook.com/Angel.Martinez.author

Twitter:
https://twitter.com/#!/AngelMartinezrr

Blog:
http://www.freewebs.com/angelwrites/apps/blog/

Email:
ravenesperanza@yahoo.com

FINN
ENDANGERED FAE 1
ANGEL MARTINEZ

INCLUDES THE BONUS READ
FINN'S CHRISTMAS

SILVER PUBLISHING
Published by Silver Publishing
Publisher of Erotic Romance

If you purchased this book without a cover you should be aware that this book is stolen property. It was reported as "unsold and destroyed" to the publisher, and neither the author nor the publisher has received any payment for this "stripped book."

SILVERPUBLISHING

ISBN 978-1-61495-644-0

Endangered Fae 1: Finn
Endangered Fae 1.5: Finn's Christmas
Copyright © 2011 by Angel Martinez
Cover Artist: Reese Dante

All rights reserved. Except for use in any review, the reproduction or utilization of this work in whole or in part in any form by any electronic, mechanical or other means, now known or hereafter invented, including xerography, photocopying and recording, or in any information storage or retrieval system, is forbidden without the written permission of the editorial office, Silver Publishing, 18530 Mack Avenue, Box 253, Grosse Pointe Farms, MI 48236, USA.

All characters in this book have no existence outside the imagination of the author and have no relation whatsoever to anyone bearing the same name or names. They are not even distantly inspired by any individual known or unknown to the author, and all incidents are pure invention.

Visit Silver Publishing at https://spsilverpublishing.com

Note from the Publisher

Dear Reader,

Thank you for your purchase of this title. The authors and staff of Silver Publishing hope you enjoy this read and that we will have a long and happy association together.

Please remember that the only money authors make from writing comes from the sales of their books. If you like their work, spread the word and tell others about the books, but please refrain from copying this book in any form. Authors depend on sales and sales only to support their families.

If you see "free shares" offered or cut-rate sales of this title on ebook pirate sites, you can report the offending entry to copyright@spsilverpublishing.com.

Thank you for not pirating our titles.

Lodewyk Deysel
Publisher
Silver Publishing
http://www.spsilverpublishing.com

Dedication

To all the brave women who came before, from Mary Shelley to C. J. Cherryh, this book is dedicated in heartfelt thanks. You paved the way in a boys' world and lent us the courage to write what was in our hearts.

Trademarks Acknowledgement

The author acknowledges the trademarked status and trademark owners of the following wordmarks mentioned in this work of fiction:

Fedex: Federal Express Corporation

Chapter 1: Rescuing Finn

The figure crouched on the bridge shocked Diego so thoroughly he drove a hundred yards before he realized what he had seen.

A man squatted on his heels on the rail, one hand on a cable, the other clutching a ragged blanket at his throat. Threadbare cloth flapped around bare ankles. The persistent wind yanked it this way and that to show flashes of naked legs.

"Holy shit," Diego muttered, as he wrestled his ancient Toyota into the nearest side street to park. This was none of his business. Didn't he have enough problems? Even as he argued with himself, he ran, dodging traffic and ignoring angry epithets as he pelted back up the bridge against traffic. The inevitable gaper delay had slowed the flow at least, making his precarious journey easier.

People stared from the safety of their vehicles as they inched along but no one stopped to help.

Diego ignored them. His primary concern was not to startle the man into falling. He slowed his approach, ready to offer soothing words, but the man heard his footsteps. Long black hair whipped and snaked in the wind, hiding his face, though Diego caught a glimpse of bared teeth.

"Did you come after me?" the jumper snarled. "I won't go back."

"Go back where?" Diego seized the opportunity to start the man talking.

The jumper shook his head to clear the hair from his eyes and peered at Diego. Black eyes, not dark brown, but black, set in deeply shadowed sockets. "No, I suppose you don't look like one of those," he said in a softly accented, weary voice.

"One of who?" Diego edged closer to

stand next to him.

"The ones who shut me in the iron cage. I changed. I escaped." His words seemed to stick in his throat and even above the traffic, Diego heard him swallow hard. "But now I'm too tired. I can't... and the river is so filthy. I think it might kill me."

At least he doesn't sound like he wants to die. "Look, if you don't want the police catching up to you, or the hospital staff, or whoever it is, this is about the worst thing you could do. You're upsetting all these people and attracting a lot of attention. They'll be here any minute." Diego reached out a hand, palm up. "Please come down. Let's get you safe and out of the wind. Then we'll see about straightening all this out."

The man regarded him through the shifting curtain of hair for a long moment. "What are you called?"

Depends who you talk to. "My name is

Diego. Diego Sandoval." He lurched forward when the man swayed, his stomach plummeting to his feet, but the jumper retained his place on the rail.

The man repeated his name a few times as if trying it out and then nodded. "It's a good name. Pleasurable to say."

"And you?"

"I am called Fionnachd."

Diego tried to repeat it and won a hint of a smile from the man when he mangled the pronunciation. "Could I call you Finn?"

That got a shrug. The blanket fell back from his shoulder to reveal all too prominent bones. "You could. Some have. I don't mind."

"Climb down, Finn," Diego urged again. "I'll help you. Let's get you somewhere quiet where you can rest."

Finn took his fingers in a light grip and Diego caught a whiff of rotten orange rinds as he slid from the rail.

What the hell am I doing? He could have Hepatitis or HIV or tuberculosis, or worse. He's probably crazy. Maybe even dangerous.

The intense plea in those black-on-black eyes silenced his practical objections. Lost and alone, he needed someone. Diego had never been good at walking away.

He slipped out of his trench coat, placed it around Finn's shoulders, followed it with his arm and led him away. His 'latest project', Mitch would have sneered. Not that he should care any more what Mitch thought.

They reached the car without incident, but here, Finn balked. "They put me in one of those before."

One of... the car? "Well, I doubt it was as beat up as this one," Diego tried to joke, but Finn backed a step. Diego patted the car's roof. "No lights. Not a police car. Or an ambulance."

Finn lifted his chin and sniffed the air. "You do smell kind and trustworthy. But some of the others did, too."

"They probably wanted to help you and didn't know what would upset you. Why did they arrest you? Did they say?"

Finn rubbed a hand over the side of his head, further snarling the mess of hair over the top half of his face. "Indecent exposure. I don't know what's indecent about standing on the dock watching the boats, though."

Irish. Diego was certain he'd placed the accent. "It's usually because someone's stark naked, not because they're watching boats."

"Oh."

He had no idea how much of this was a put on. No one could be that naïve. Though someone could be that deluded. Time enough to sort it all out later. Right now, he had to get Finn off the street before he crumpled to the pavement.

"Look, this goes both ways. I don't know if I can trust you either," Diego said, as he opened the passenger door.

A Cheshire Cat grin bloomed under the flying mass of hair. "Well said. You may be the first sensible person I've met since I woke."

Finn took the two steps to the car and let Diego help him in. He gingerly avoided touching the doorframe but finally settled back with an exhausted sigh.

Diego drove away just as sirens began to sound on the bridge.

* * * *

The ordeal of the shower seemed cruel, but Finn was filthy and smelled like a dumpster during a garbage strike. Diego placed one of his plastic kitchen chairs in the middle of the shower and installed Finn there, but he only slumped against the chair back, eyes closed, face turned into the spray.

Too exhausted to even flinch.

Diego fought down the little shiver of revulsion at the stench, stripped to his boxers, and stepped into the stall with him. He attacked the tangled mass of hair first, positioning Finn so his head hung back over the chair. No lice—a good sign. He might have been homeless, but he probably hadn't lived on the streets too long. The nest of midnight snarls unwound under the caress of water and shampoo. If Finn stood, his hair would reach at least to the top curve of his butt. A strange blue-black iridescence shone in it, his natural coloring as far as Diego could tell rather than bottled special effects.

The rest Diego washed with a loofah, shoving away modesty out of a need to get Finn to his rest. An ache lodged around his heart to see how malnutrition had ravaged what probably had been a lean-muscled frame. An athlete, perhaps, before he went off the deep end, an impression reinforced by the absence of almost all body hair. Waxed or electrolysis-denuded—only Finn's crotch sported a black thatch of soft hair. Swimmer, perhaps. The Olympic competitors often shaved it all off for every small gain in streamlining.

He turned off the water and tugged at Finn's arm. "Come on. Let's get you settled. You can't sleep in the shower."

Finn staggered to his feet and Diego all but carried him to Mitch's room. The spare room, he corrected himself. He usually kept the door closed so the stark, unfurnished space wasn't glaring at him.

He sat Finn down against the wall, brought him a pair of flannel pajamas, soft with age, and went out to the front closet to retrieve the air mattress and vacuum. Six boxes lay stacked against the wall; all that remained of Mitch's things. Diego ran a hand over one, and then shook his head against the temptation to open the top and look over its contents. When he returned, Finn hadn't moved from where he sat naked and dozing in a patch of sunlight.

"You might want to put those on." Diego toed the pajamas closer as he dragged the air mattress into place. When Finn's only response was a long sigh, he added, "We need to get you warm. I don't want to have to take you to Emergency."

With a puzzled frown, Finn unfolded the material and managed, after looking back and forth between the pajamas and Diego's jeans a few times, to pull the bottoms on. His efforts with the top, though, were sabotaged when the vacuum roared to life. He startled and scuttled sideways, wide-eyed and panting.

Diego hurried to switch it off. "Sorry. Should have warned you."

"Is it some sort of small dragon?"

For a moment, Diego stared in blank surprise before he caught himself. At least the nature of Finn's delusion was becoming clearer. He might even share his history later when he had the energy, perhaps some tragic story of an exiled prince. For now, Diego thought it best to play along.

"Not a dragon. Just a machine. It blows out and sucks in air with great force."

"Ah." Finn seemed disappointed, but waved a hand for him to continue.

Mattress inflated, Finn dressed and installed in bed, Diego thought he should get something in him before he drifted off. He tried tap water first but Finn jerked his head away, the color draining from his face.

"Tainted," he gasped. "Great Dagda, it reeks."

Diego sniffed above the glass, puzzled. New York City water, piped in from the mountains, was cleaner than most but it was treated. Chlorine. Fluoride. Maybe Finn had an allergy to one or the other.

Bottled water produced a less violent reaction. Finn smelled it, nose crinkled, but he downed half the bottle in desperate gulps before Diego could take it back from him. Hydration, at least, wouldn't be an issue.

The hurdle of food remained. Starvation often did terrible things to the body's ability to accept nourishment. Not the best time to offer a hamburger and fries. Diego decided he should start with the foods one was supposed to give sick kids: bananas, rice, applesauce and toast, minus the applesauce, since he didn't have any.

Finn wouldn't touch the boiled-in-tap-water rice. He nibbled a corner of the toast and set it aside with murmured apologies. The banana completely stumped him. He turned it over and over in his hands and finally tried to bite through the skin.

"You eat these?" He handed it back to Diego with a grimace.

All right, so his reality doesn't include New World fruit. Diego peeled the banana for him and handed it back. "You don't eat the skin.

Try the inside."

He took a careful bite and his eyes widened. "That's not bad."

Diego could only watch anxiously, praying his guest wouldn't choke, as the rest disappeared in three bites. With a contented sigh, Finn handed the peel back, gathered the covers into a circle in the center of the mattress, and curled into a tight ball inside his nest. By the time Diego brought an extra comforter to cover him, Finn was fast asleep.

Clean and at rest, his face had a childlike quality with his hair tucked behind one finely-curved ear. Diego wasn't certain it was a handsome face, almost unearthly in its delicacy, and though Finn stood six inches taller, he had the odd feeling he could scoop that long frame up in his arms without much effort.

He backed out and closed the door as quietly as he could, confident Finn wouldn't die on him. Tomorrow he would see about finding the right agency to take his guest, preferably one that wouldn't hand him right over to immigration.

A few hours of peace while Finn slept should let him at least get through the current chapter.

The moment he sat ready at his desk, fingers poised over the keys, the phone rang.

Chapter 2: Mitch

"Hey."

Diego felt as if a tourniquet tightened around his throat. "Mitch… how are you?"

"Good."

In the long silence, he thought of dozens of things he should say. None of them made it out.

"Look." Mitch's voice edged toward annoyance. "I'm coming over to get the rest of my stuff. I don't want any scenes. No drama. Okay?"

"All right." Diego heard himself speaking from far away. "Could we maybe talk about this?"

"Stop it. We had fun. It's over."

"Not for me it's not," Diego whispered, resting his forehead on the desk.

"I'm on my way. Don't make this uglier than it has to be."

"Now?"

"Yes, now. Jesus, Diego. You have somewhere important you have to be?" The note of contempt stung more than harsh words ever could.

"I'll be here."

The last straw, two weeks before, had been so petty but everything had been too far gone by then. Diego pulled a four-week-old kitten out of a dumpster. Normally Mitch would have rolled his eyes or offered some caustic remark and let it go at that, but they had been dressed to the nines, on the way to a party given by one of Mitch's business associates.

"Shit, Diego! It's filthy. Put it back." Even in the dim alley, he had seen Mitch's face turn crimson.

"She needs help," Diego pleaded. "I'll take her to rescue, go change, and meet you there. I won't be long."

"You come with me now or don't bother

showing up." Mitch had spoken in a calm, reasonable tone. It wasn't until the next morning when he still hadn't come home that Diego realized he'd received an ultimatum for more than just the evening. He'd chosen a skinny, flea-ridden castoff over his handsome lover for the last time.

He wandered out into the hall to run his fingertips over the stacked boxes. All so lovingly packed; why had he bothered? What was he expecting Mitch to say? 'Oh, Diego, thank you for going to all this trouble. I'm sorry I ever left you. I'll be home tonight.'

Mitch's hands sliding down his ribs, full lips tracing patterns along his throat...

Diego shivered and closed his eyes, an endless chasm opening under his feet. "God." He slapped a hand on the wall to steady himself. Carbamazepine... had he taken it this morning?

Three years and it all came down to a few boxes and a bedroom set. Plans for a life together, the house in Connecticut—all sand through his fingers.

"The whole world comes first for you," Mitch declared one night during a bitter argument. "The bag lady down the street. The junkie on the corner. Some damn alley cat. Any excuse to shove me to the side."

Diego could offer no defense to what was only truth. Not that he wanted to shove Mitch aside, but the need to help was a compulsion, almost an addiction.

Under different circumstances, the seizures might have brought them closer again as shared trauma sometimes will. But they were his own doing in Mitch's eyes; one more crime Diego had committed to sabotage their relationship.

His faint hopes of having one more chance to talk to Mitch face to face were dashed when he opened the door. Two young men accompanied him, vaguely familiar. They'd probably met at one party or another.

"You remember Chad and Michael," Mitch said as he strode in. Cursory greetings were offered all around, no one quite willing to meet anyone's eyes. Mitch proceeded to look over the boxes as if this were the most normal thing in the world. "This everything?"

Stunned, Diego managed a nod.

"Where are my clubs?"

Oh, damn, the golf clubs. "They're still in the bedroom closet. I'll—"

"Don't bother." Mitch shoved past him. "I'll get them."

"Mitch, don't..."

"Holy crap! What the hell?"

Diego cringed and hurried in to place himself between Mitch and Finn. "Sh, please. He's a friend. He's sick. Please don't disturb him."

"Right. Sure. Look, he's either more than 'just a friend' since he's sleeping in your pj's and you've been lying out your ass about how broken up you've been. Or he's the kind of 'friend' who usually lives in a cardboard box and you're lying to me about taking in a junkie. Christ, Diego. Aren't you ever going to learn?"

"It's not as if it was your room anymore."

Mitch snorted. "No, but half my stuff's still here. And one of these days, one of your projects will kill you in your sleep. Same old shit. Never changes. No matter how many times you promise, or how many times you get hurt."

Diego's face burned. "It was just that once. I misjudged."

"You got the crap beat out of you. Comatose, for chrissakes!"

"Maybe if you'd stayed—"

"Don't hand me that. You hide behind this charitable shit so you don't have to look at the mess your life is in." Mitch grabbed his clubs out of the closet and slammed the door.

Finn didn't twitch, but one black eye gleamed through his forest of hair.

"Get a fucking job like everyone else. Or stop sulking about rejections and get serious. How many novels have you really finished?"

Two. Well, one. And most of another.

"Is your agent sick of you yet?"

"I thought you didn't want this to get ugly," Diego said, arms wrapped tightly around his ribs. He edged out of the bedroom, hoping Mitch would follow. "Not everything's about money, Mitch. Or about you."

"Go ahead. Twist everything around. That's what you're best at." Mitch stormed back into the front room. "I always harped on you because I worried about you. But I've had enough of watching you waste your life. I even set up that interview at the Times for you. Remember? No, you couldn't be bothered."

"I didn't—"

"Whatever. Journalism's beneath you or

something. So you rely on freelance shit and hope you'll have the rent next month and don't have any damn health insurance. Know what I think?" Mitch whirled on him, closing the distance to snarl in his face. "I think you like being a loser. I think there's some bizarre romantic attachment to it. Like you're fucking Jack Kerouac or something. Well, you're not. And you never will be."

The boxes had all disappeared, whisked away by Mitch's helpers. Diego swallowed hard, panic setting in. Mitch was about to walk out again. His gorge rose as the scent of rotting meat filled his nostrils. *Not now. Oh, please, God, not now.*

"Call me when you finally sell something." Mitch slung the golf bag onto his shoulder as he headed for the door. "Like that'll ever happen."

"Mitch!" Diego tried to go after him but the air in the room had grown too thick. The door slammed and the world exploded in a thousand crackling shards of glass.

Chapter 3: Odd Reactions

Soft. Bed? Footsteps nearby. Muted clink of dishes. Cooking smells. Cumin, Chili. Mama?

No, she was gone. Years ago.

Pain edged into his back and his joints. His hip stabbed at him. Someone had overstuffed his head with cotton batting until it threatened to burst. A low moan escaped before he could open his eyes.

"Diego? *Despiertos*?"

The voice percolated through the fuzz in his brain and took on an identity. "*Si, Tia Carmen*. I'm awake." Not him, that scraggly rasp. Couldn't be.

"*Bueno*. That wasn't so long."

Tia Carmen's face hovered above him. Teacup. Aspirin. Diego blinked, trying to pull the disparate images into a less disorienting whole. He took another moment to resolve the usual idiotic questions himself. What happened? Grand mal. Where am I? Living room sofa.

"When did you get here?"

She perched beside him, her white hair luminous in the lamplight. "I heard drumming on my ceiling. I thought 'Diego is either having a tantrum or a stroke'."

"Seizure," he corrected absently. *Though I might have both at once someday.*

"Yes, yes." She patted his arm. "So the door was unlocked and your friend was with you—"

"Mitch?"

She snorted. "That one? No. The sick one with the pretty hair. He was crawling on the floor shoving furniture away from you."

Diego's head snapped around to search for him, the movement knifing pain behind his eyes.

"I put him back to bed." She rested an arthritis-gnarled hand on his chest to keep him down. "With a plate of *platanos*."

"Is that good for him? Fried food? I don't think he's eaten in a long time."

She gave him a look, at once imperious and amused. "And how many children have you raised, *niño*? He liked them. He ate them. Let him eat what he wants right now." She rose, smoothing her skirt. "Dinner will be ready in an hour. Try to sleep."

"Tia Carmen? I'm sorry."

"Shush." She flapped a dismissive hand at him. "Don't be sorry for needing help. Everyone needs help sometimes. So someone told me."

Diego managed a wry smile at having his words thrown back at him. He downed the aspirin, and as he sipped his tea, her words slid through his jumbled brain. Finn, sick as he was, had dragged himself out of bed to help. He couldn't begin to contemplate what that meant yet.

And how had he gotten on the sofa?

He woke later to the sound of dishes being set down near his ear. Finn sat cross-legged on the floor at one end of the coffee table, already wolfing down a portion of *mole*-smothered enchiladas.

"Your stomach's going to hate you."

Finn put down the plate and wiped his chin on his sleeve. "Evening. Feeling better?"

"I will in the morning. And you? You seem... livelier."

"This lovely lady's cooking has amazing restorative powers." His hair was brushed to gleaming and pulled back in a black elastic, most likely Tia Carmen's doing. "That nasty churl was your lover?"

Diego levered himself up against the cushions, nausea fighting hunger. "Was. Yes."

Finn shook his head and returned to devouring his dinner. "Can't say much for your tastes. Anyone who'd run off while his friend has an attack of the falling sickness... a right bastard."

"I told him this, many times." Tia Carmen settled in the wing chair to his left. "He never listens to me."

Wonderful. My landlady and my bridge jumper have formed an alliance. "I'd like to take you down to the clinic tomorrow, Finn," he said, to change the subject. "Get you checked out."

Finn cocked his head to one side like a puzzled bird. "Checked out?"

"Let the doctors run some tests. To see if you're sick."

"I need a doctor to tell me?" Finn grumbled around a mouthful of enchilada. "Poisoned air. Poisoned water. Of course I'm sick."

"Eat your dinner, Diego." Tia Carmen handed a plate over. "Finn will go with you to the clinic, won't you, *caro*? To make Diego happy?"

A white-toothed grin replaced the scowl. "Did I say no? For my hero, I will go to whatever this place is."

Tia Carmen laughed and Diego concentrated on his food to hide his embarrassment. Odd. He was hungry after all.

* * * *

Finding clothes for Finn proved easy. Mitch had left enough cast-offs in the front closet from which to choose, three bags Diego hadn't had the chance to take to the mission yet. Though Finn was far lankier and at least two inches taller than Mitch, a pair of old track pants and a stretched-out sweatshirt fit well enough. There was even an ankle-length, black leather coat Mitch had declared 'too Goth' a week after purchasing it.

Shoes, however, posed a problem.

Finn's feet couldn't be shoved into

Mitch's old sneakers. He tried to curl his long, elegant toes under to make it work, but gave up the effort when he realized how painful that would be. They finally had to settle for a pair of flip-flops, not quite the right size, but at least only the ends of his toes hung off the front.

"We'll find you something better today," Diego reassured him. "The Goodwill on Fulton always has shoes. Are you up for a walk? It's about four blocks to the clinic and I'll probably be making some stops along the way."

"Blocks?" Finn tilted his head like a puzzled bird.

"Never mind." Diego shrugged into his jacket. "It'll take us about twenty, thirty minutes to get there. You feel well enough? Or should I call a cab and forget the stops?"

Finn pulled in a slow breath, as if assessing his lung capacity. "It's better today. I believe I'll manage."

"You'll tell me if you feel tired or

woozy?"

"My word of honor." Finn tapped a finger against his heart, an odd smile twitching at his lips.

Tia Carmen poked her head out as they clattered down the stairs. "Diego? Could I contribute today?"

He stopped to kiss her cheek. "If you want to. Just a couple dollars, though. I'm doing all right today."

She handed him a five and he knew better than to argue. "Don't keep him out too long in this cold," she admonished, though it wasn't clear whether she meant Diego or Finn.

Outside, Finn's head twisted this way and that as taxis and bicycle messengers whizzed by. He appeared more interested than frightened, though he did edge closer to Diego when a bus roared past.

"Best to watch where you're walking." Diego grabbed his sleeve to steer him clear of a fire hydrant.

Finn nodded, though his head kept swiveling, his nostrils flared. A skateboarder zipping by, the rumble of the subway under a grate, a woman laughing as she spoke on her cell, the chestnut vendor across the street—every sight, sound and scent tore his attention in a thousand directions.

"Here's George," Diego offered, hoping to provide some momentary focus. He indicated the pretzel cart at the corner. "He's our first stop."

"Morning, Hemingway!" George waved from under his umbrella. "How many today?"

"Ten, I think." Diego dug in his pockets to gather enough change. "Finn might want one."

"That your new friend's name?"

"Yes. George, this is Finn. Finn, George Stanakopoulis."

"Honored," Finn said, and offered a

theatrical bow.

George laughed. "Not from around here, is he?"

"No." Diego nudged Finn. "We don't, ah, greet people that way. Usually."

"Oh, I don't mind," George said. "Neighborhood could use a little class." He bagged up the pretzels and handed one to Finn.

To Diego's enormous relief, the pretzel absorbed all of Finn's attention as they walked. He turned it this way and that, sniffed it a few times and licked it.

"Do you eat all of the salt?"

"You don't have to. It brushes right off."

Finn nibbled a corner and grimaced. "The things you people consume."

"Put it in your pocket. Maybe we'll stop on the way home and feed the birds."

"Pockets," Finn mused as he stuffed the pretzel in his coat pocket. "Ingenious invention. I've always thought them the only legitimate reason for wearing clothes."

"Hey, D-man!" A bundle of cardboard and wool called from the sidewalk.

"Josh. Where's Tiff?" Diego crouched down where he could see the too-young face peering out under a mop of brown hair and handed over a pretzel. Runaways. Sometimes he could coax them into the shelters, sometimes they refused.

"She's gone to, y'know, freshen up." Josh snickered and attacked the pretzel with gusto.

"It'll be single digits tonight. Make sure you get inside, please."

"Yeah, yeah, okay, Mom."

"You might make it. Tiff and the baby she's carrying won't. At least say you'll go to the mission."

That got through. Josh shot him a guilty look, grumbled something unintelligible and disappeared under the blankets with Tiff's pretzel.

"Everyone else simply goes by the ones on the walkway," Finn said after a few more stops. "Or walks over them. And they don't seem to notice anyone either. Except you."

Diego shrugged. "I think it's important to know your neighbors."

Finn regarded him for a long moment. "How charmingly naïve. You've no idea what you are."

And what am I? Diego kept this to himself, fairly certain he didn't want the answer.

"Holding up all right?"

"Well enough." Finn rubbed at his chest. "One could wish to draw a full breath."

"Almost there. Just need to see if Rodney's home."

Rodney West lived in the alley across the street from the clinic. His domicile consisted of cardboard and cloth, corrugated pipe and plastic sheeting. Every inch crawled with complex designs and figures of symbolic significance made with any medium Rodney could find—leftover paint, pen, charcoal, crayons, colored bits of food wrappers and bottle tops. The History, he called this indecipherable work, though Diego never got it quite clear whether the title referred to a history long past or an ongoing one, or one describing an apocalyptic vision of the future.

"Wait here a sec." Diego stopped Finn ten feet from the wild construction. "We have to follow certain steps to see him."

He picked up an empty can and rolled it toward the door, its hollow rattle serving as doorbell and alarm.

"Who's out there?" A bass so deep it could have originated from the center of the Earth rumbled from the shelter.

"It's Diego. Original and unaltered. Accept no substitutions." Rodney insisted on this formula to prove identity. Otherwise, apparently, Diego could have been a government clone or under coercion by some shadowy, threatening agency.

A corner of cloth lifted, a bloodshot eye peered out, and the artist emerged as far as his doorframe-wide shoulders. "Diego. You don't look well."

"Seizure last night. I'm just tired." Diego closed the distance to crouch by Rodney's door.

"Who's that?" Rodney pointed with his chin.

"This is Finn." Diego waved him closer and Finn joined him by the door, examining the artwork in his curious-bird way.

"And where'd he come from?"

"The valiant Diego pulled me off the bridge. The Brook Lynn Bridge? Do I have that right?"

Rodney's laugh boomed deeper than his voice. "True to form, our Diego—" He cut off abruptly, and his hand shot out to seize Finn by the forearm. "But where did you come from?

You don't belong here."

"Please…" Finn pulled back, his pale complexion edging toward gray.

"I know you. You're one of them. From the Other Place. But not one of the Dark. No. You're different. Stay out of the tunnels. They lurk there. They'll eat your soul. Drink your songs into blackness. Not from here. They'd want you…"

"Rodney, let him go!" Diego said in alarm, as Finn dug his heels in and struggled backward.

Finn jerked away and backpedaled to the mouth of the alley, panting.

"Maybe not the best way to make friends." Diego shook his head. "Scaring the hell out of people."

"He needs to be scared," Rodney declared, and disappeared into his home.

"Finn?"

He stood with his arms wrapped around

himself and backed another step as Diego approached. For a moment, a trick of the light made those black eyes gleam red, anger and suspicion radiating from them.

"I'm sorry," Diego offered, hands spread. "He's not having one of his more lucid days. He's not dangerous, though. He wouldn't hurt you."

Finn relaxed with a slow intake of breath. "No, you couldn't have known. I forgive you."

They endured the usual hour wait at the clinic, but Finn behaved, amusing himself with magazine pictures, asking Diego for explanations from time to time. He knew nothing about the trouble in the Middle East or US politics, and the entire concept of 'movies' had to be explained when he reached a picture of Cate Blanchett.

"We need a last name for you," Diego murmured, as he struggled through the necessary forms for Finn, who seemed illiterate. "If you don't want to give me your real one, fine. Make one up. Maybe the name of the town you came from or something."

Deeply engrossed in a full-page ad for Calvin Klein underwear, Finn needed a nudge and a repetition of the request.

"Shannon," he said, rolling the word out, unmistakable longing in his voice. He stared across the room, thousands of miles away, then shook his head and returned to his pictures.

Shannon, Finn, Diego wrote in the appropriate spaces. For address and phone number, he filled in his own. Finn pretended incomprehension regarding date of birth, so he concocted one of those as well, estimating Finn at about twenty-eight or so. Social security, insurance information, previous address, and medical history all remained stubbornly blank.

A nurse in powder blue scrubs emerged from the back holding a chart and shaking her head. "Now tell me how I knew this was one of yours, sugarpie."

Diego smiled as he rose. "*Hola*, Rita. You recognized my handwriting?"

"More like the pitiful white spaces on the forms. At least this one's cleaner. You staying with him?"

"If I could, please."

"I don't know how that skinny body of yours has room for your heart. Come on back."

She showed them to an examination room and had Finn strip to the waist. The first sign of trouble came when she tried to strap on the blood pressure cuff. Finn yanked his arm away and scooted toward the wall.

Diego put a hand on his shoulder. "It's all right. Rita just wants to measure how well your heart's working. Rita, Finn seems to be stuck in the wrong century. Maybe if you tell him what you're doing beforehand?"

"Here, hon, give me your arm. Attaboy."

Rita tried again with better success.

"You have the most lovely skin," Finn told her. "Like mahogany. Like the finest river loam. Could I touch it?"

"You are touching it, Casanova," Rita answered, eyes on the blood pressure dial. "Behave."

"Casanova?" Finn shot Diego a questioning glance.

"Famous lover."

"Ah. A compliment?"

"Sarcasm." *Please don't make me explain sarcasm.*

"Typical."

Apparently, it wouldn't be necessary.

The doctor, one of a long string of resentful young people just out of residency, never the same one twice, conducted a cursory examination. After a few snide remarks about having enough indigent people in the country without having to import them, he ordered blood drawn.

"I don't understand why you're conscious, Mr Shannon, with vitals this low." He flipped through the chart as he left the room. "Full workup, Rita."

Finn's eyes were round in alarm. "What does he mean, drawing blood? Has he issued challenge? I don't think he liked me much."

"No, no," Diego hurried to explain. "He just wants them to take a little blood from you for some tests. It's not the most pleasant thing in the world but it won't harm you. They put a needle in your arm, but just for a minute. It's not enough blood you'd ever notice."

"Oh." Finn looked far from reassured.

Diego's heart sank when the phlebotomist arrived, the dour, unfriendly one. An orderly approximately the size of a VW accompanied her.

"Please, that's not necessary," Diego pleaded when they rolled the heavy cart over and strapped Finn's arm to the attached board.

"Mr Sandoval, step out into the hall if you're going to be a nuisance," the woman snapped.

"Sorry." Diego retreated out of the way. "It'll be okay, Finn. Look at me. Don't watch. Just be a minute."

Despite his efforts at distraction, Finn's reactions swiftly deteriorated from disturbed to panicked. "Diego?" he called out, in an odd, back-throat growl.

"Relax, Finn, please…"

The orderly caught him in a bear hug to pin his free arm and hold him still. The needle plunged in. Finn let out a horrific scream, more wildcat than human. The sluggish flow of too-bright red filled one vial, then two, while Finn thrashed and struggled. A sudden twist of that long body, quick as a cobra strike, and the orderly lay gasping on the floor. Finn ripped the straps and the needle from his arm. The phlebotomist rushed into the hallway to call for help. With an anguished sound, Finn clutched his arm to his chest and staggered to the door.

He turned in the doorway, leaning on the frame. Diego could have sworn flames leaped in those accusing eyes.

"Accursed humans! I thought you were different! Gods of the waters, what a great fool I've been."

"Finn—"

"Don't touch me!" Finn bared his teeth. His sides heaved, sweat plastered his hair to his forehead, and Diego thought for a moment he might faint. Instead, Finn whirled and ran.

"*Dios*," Diego whispered, grabbed up the coat and shirt Finn had been wearing and rushed after him.

No sign of him in the hall or the waiting room, though the frightened faces confirmed his passage. Diego dashed out to the street. On the sidewalk, in a pile as if Finn had melted into the sidewalk, lay the track pants, the flip flops and the boxers Diego had lent him. Finn had vanished.

He cast about for anyone who might have been watching. Across the street, Rodney peered out from his house.

"Rodney! Did you see Finn? Which way did he run?"

"I saw a great black bird. Black as the passage between the worlds. Wings the size of Atlantean cruisers. It's come to that."

Of all the times for Rodney to be having an episode. Diego gathered up the discarded clothes and hurried on. He searched alleyways and basement wells, doorways and fire escapes, asking everyone he knew. No one had seen him.

How does a six-and-a-half-foot, naked man disappear?

Finally, a thought hit him. Perhaps Finn had gone to Tia Carmen. He dashed back home and knocked frantically on her door.

"*No, querido, lo siento.*" Tia Carmen shook her head sadly. "He has not been here. I will watch for him, though."

Diego trudged upstairs to his own place, hopes of finding Finn inside dashed the moment he opened the door. The rooms had the hollow, lonely feel of an empty apartment. No sign that Finn had been there.

He called the police stations, the hospitals, and the shelters. Nothing.

Head in his hands, Diego slumped on the sofa, watching the shadows lengthen and broaden into evening. Finn would die out there that night and he was helpless to prevent it.

Chapter 4: Not a Leprechaun

Diego jerked awake. He'd dozed off after returning heartsick and exhausted from one last, futile search.

The knock sounded again. The door?

A nightmare-white face stared through his window. He shot from the bed. "Holy shit!"

Finn. How the hell?

He must have climbed the fire escape. Diego's heart leaped, and then the fear returned. Finn's last words to him, that feral snarl. What if he'd come back with murder in mind?

Finn pawed at the glass like a cat, and now that the sleep-muddled moment of nightmare retreated, Diego could observe his actual expression. Pain. Uncertainty.

He flicked on the light and threw open the window to half-support, half-drag Finn over the sill.

"Dammit, where have you been?"

"I tried…" Finn blinked and swallowed hard. "I tried to leave this cursed city. It goes on into eternity. There's no end to it. I've nowhere else to go."

Diego shoved the wild hair from his face. "You're burning up. What happened? At the clinic? What was all that?"

"They stabbed me with iron." Finn held out his arm, the collection site an angry red, his arm swollen from wrist to elbow. "Iron, Diego. It still hurts."

He sat Finn down on the edge of the bed. "Good God. She must have used a dirty needle or something."

Finn let out a short bark of laughter. "You are the kindest man I've ever met. But also the blindest. Now I know you've no idea. I'm so sorry, Diego. I accused you falsely. Your heart shines in you like a sunbeam through diamonds. You still think I'm human, don't you?"

No idea of what? "Of course you're

human. You're not taking what Rodney said seriously, are you? Lie down. Crawl under the blankets. I'll get some ice for your arm."

When Diego came back, Finn had curled up on top of the blankets. He shivered so hard the bed rattled, though the heat radiating from him could have baked a soufflé.

"I should get you to the ER. A doctor should—"

"No!" Finn grabbed his arm and yanked him down on the bed beside him. "No more human doctors. Sit still, boyo. It's time you heard the truth. I owe you that much."

"If you're an escaped murderer or something, I don't think I want to hear it."

"I'm from Eire. Ireland now, I hear."

"I knew that much."

"Just listen..." Finn clenched his teeth, his eyes squeezed shut. "Cursed, nasty, vicious... Dagda's balls, it hurts!"

Diego covered him with the comforter

and stroked his back until he could speak again.

"Somewhere close to seven hundred years ago, I was betrayed. Wounded. Heartsore. I retreated into the Dreaming and slept away the centuries, my body cradled by my beloved Shannon." Finn stopped and seized Diego's wrist in a painful grip. "You don't believe me."

"It's a little hard to swallow," Diego admitted softly. "You don't look much over twenty-five and sleeping underwater?"

"I'm not human. You have to get that through your skull before any of this will make sense. I'm one of the fae. The people who inhabited Ireland before humans came."

Diego couldn't help a nervous laugh. "Are you telling me you're a leprechaun?"

Finn shoved him so hard he fell off the bed. "No, I'm not a bleeding leprechaun! Are you completely daft? Everyone knows they don't exist."

"Sorry. Well, what are you then?" Diego

muttered as he picked himself up.

"A pooka."

Oh, yes, much more believable than a leprechaun. "Ah. Aren't pookas sort of like poltergeists?"

Finn hid his face in the pillow.

"Never mind. We'll talk about it in the morning. You need anything?"

A shake of that black-maned head.

"You want me to stay with you?"

"Please," came the muffled response. Diego slid under the blankets, leaving Finn on top of them. After a few moments, Finn shifted over to nestle his head in the hollow of Diego's shoulder. Caught off guard, Diego wondered if he should say something or move away. In the end, he did neither. Finn had fallen asleep.

* * * *

"Yes, he's here." Diego took the phone

into the front room, trying not to wake Finn.

"*Está bien?*" Clanks and clatters told him Tia Carmen was in her kitchen, phone tucked under her chin while she cooked.

"More or less. He's not well, but at least he's alive."

"*Gracias a dios.* I will come to see you later."

Diego ran a hand over his face and debated taking a short nap. Finn had tossed and muttered most of the night. Instead, he powered up his computer and searched out everything he could regarding pookas.

There was precious little to be found and much of that was contradictory. They were mischievous sprites who delighted in breaking crockery and knocking fences over. They were guardian river spirits who appeared to people as black horses with flaming eyes to entice the unwary into a ride and then dump them in the swamp. They were vengeful fae, resentful of human encroachment, and prone to violent reprisals.

Ghost, woodland deity, fairy, monster—no two accounts agreed on the nature of the legendary creature. But at least none of the websites called them leprechauns.

A soft knock at the door heralded Tia Carmen's arrival. He hurried out to greet her.

"He's still sleeping," he whispered.

"*Pobre niño*," she murmured, as she handed Diego the cardboard box she carried. Wonderful, complex smells rose from under the cover of dishtowels. He jerked his head toward the kitchen where he placed the box on the counter.

"He thinks he's a pooka."

"Pooka?" Tia Carmen's white eyebrows nearly disappeared when her forehead crinkled.

"*Un hada de Irlanda*, an Irish fairy," Diego explained. "Though 'leprechaun' offends him somehow."

She only nodded as she unpacked plastic containers from the box.

"You don't seem surprised."

"I am too old to be surprised." She shrugged. "You must have noticed strange things about him."

"Please don't tell me you believe him."

Her hands stopped in the middle of folding the towels into precise squares. "For a smart man, Santiago, you are sometimes a little heavy."

"Dense," Diego corrected automatically, his ears burning. An odd dislocation of time and space struck him: six years old rather than grown, standing in his *abuela's* kitchen in Miami. He sat down hard on one of the red plastic chairs. To head off her inquiries after his health, he told her about the trip to the clinic and Finn's odd return.

"*Por supuesto*, no wonder he is so sick." She pulled one of his aluminum pans out of the cabinet and poured two bottles of water into it. "*Los hadas*, iron burns them. And steel. It is poison to them."

"I know the stories, Tia Carmen. But, honestly."

"He was out on the iron fire escape last night? Have you looked at the bottoms of his feet?"

"No, but…"

She threw a handful of herbs in the water. "Tell me again what you believe after you do."

"If they're burned, it's from frostbite. It was eight degrees last night."

"*Ay*, Diego. So stubborn." She raised her eyes to the ceiling as if help might be found there.

"They are. And it wasn't the cold." Finn leaned in the doorway, white as milk. Diego leaped up to catch him before he could fall and eased him into a chair.

"Hush now, my hero, I'm well enough." Finn gave him a tired smile when Diego pulled over a second chair to prop up his feet. "Don't fuss so."

Red lines crisscrossed the soles of his feet where they had touched the frigid fire escape. "I should get you some slippers," Diego murmured.

"Are you hungry, *caro*?" Tia Carmen crossed the room to kiss the top of Finn's head.

Finn beamed at her, adoration in his eyes. "For your cooking, dear lady, I will always be hungry."

If those eyes looked at me that way... Diego cut the thought short. *Don't be an idiot.*

She had brought chicken and stuffed poblanos, red beans, and rice. The heavenly scents filled the kitchen and Finn leaned back in the chair, nostrils flared as he took in a deep breath. His forehead crinkled when she put a steaming mug of the herb brew from the stove in front of him instead of food.

"For the fever," she informed him. "Drink it down."

"Must I?" Finn sniffed at the concoction dubiously, sounding closer to ten years old than the several hundred he claimed.

"You want to eat? You take your medicine first."

Why this half-feral man obeyed Tia Carmen so meekly, Diego couldn't fathom, but every last drop of the herb tea disappeared in short order.

"When did you come here?" Diego asked while they ate. Not that he wanted to knock holes in Finn's story, but he wanted to make some sense of it all.

Deeply engrossed in making a disaster area of his poblano, Finn looked up and licked the cheese from his fingers. "The day before you found me."

"No luggage? No clothes? No passport?"

Finn turned to speak *sotto voce* to Tia Carmen. "I do believe our Diego thinks I'm a liar."

"Aren't you?" She nudged him.

"When it suits me." Finn's smile faded into a puzzled frown. "Though it's difficult to lie about things you've no inkling of."

"I'm not calling you a liar," Diego protested softly. "I'm just confused. You seem so homesick. Why did you come here?"

"For the food," Finn answered with a straight face.

Later on, when Diego saw Tia Carmen to the door, she whispered to him, "He can't stay here. You know that."

Diego stared at her in shock and then ducked his head, a flush of shame creeping up his throat. "I'm sorry. You're right. I shouldn't be taking in strange men, endangering your other tenants. I'll… I'll find him someplace as soon as possible."

She patted his arm. "I should be very angry with you for thinking me so heartless. I didn't mean he should leave your place. He may stay with you as long as he likes. But he must not stay in the city. He will never be truly well again if he does."

"You mean I can't keep him because he needs trees and grass and room to roam?" Diego forced both the smile and the joke.

"*Si, precisamente.*"

Chapter 5: Persuasive Evidence

"Dizziness, GI upset, anemia..." Diego read as he tipped out his pills for the day. The carbamazepine controlled the seizures when he remembered to take it, but it killed his appetite and forced him to take iron supplements for the anemia. No cure, his doctor said, and warned him the episodes could become more frequent, perhaps preceded by hallucinations someday. Wonderful.

He recalled nothing about the attack. Nothing about that day. His brain hid the memories from him like bean-size shards of glass in a sand dune. Even if one were to cut one's foot on a piece, the chances of finding it were slim to none.

Mitch had told him he had approached a homeless man in an alley with an offer of food and the man proved unstable. A tire iron, several blows to the head, and a prolonged hospital stay later, left Diego with holes in his memory and a seizure disorder.

"I'd like to ask a favor." Finn's soft, deep voice startled him. He'd slept on the air mattress again the night before, declaring it was more like home.

"What sort of favor?"

Finn took his hand and pulled him to the bathroom, where he pointed to the tub. "That large vessel there. I assume it holds water."

"You want a bath? Just turn the taps on like I showed you for the sink."

"I thought as much. Now for the favor I'd have of you. Could we fill it with water from the bottles?"

How many gallons in a bathtub? He should have seen this coming since Finn so despised the tap water. They sold those huge jugs of spring water at the supermarket, didn't they?

"You'll have to give me a little time on

this one. Tell you what: if you can promise to stay here and out of trouble, I'll go get some. We need groceries anyway and you still need shoes."

Finn put a hand over his heart. "I won't stray out the door. I swear."

This, coming from an admitted liar, was perhaps not the most comforting promise. Diego resolved to stop at Tia Carmen's door on his way down to ask her to keep an ear out.

"Do you have any of those smooth, shiny books with all the picture leaves?" Finn asked when Diego was on his way out.

Magazines. He never had any lying around. In a desperate attempt to find something to keep his unpredictable guest occupied, he heaved down the survey of Renaissance Art. The huge tome connected with the coffee table with a solid thud. Finn eased the cover open and soon sat entranced, giving Diego high hopes that he might come home to both Finn and apartment safe and intact.

At the Goodwill downtown, Diego found a decent pair of leather high-tops, size fourteen, and a respectable selection of clothes that would fit better than Mitch's castoffs. At the market, he puzzled over the cooler-sized water bottles and finally decided on six. Only when he reached home again and parked the car, did he realize he would have to lug them all upstairs.

"Maybe I can do two at a time," he muttered, as he stared at the sea of bottles in his trunk.

One bottle gripped in his right hand, the other slung on his left shoulder, Diego struggled up the steps. He arrived at his front door gasping and let both bottles down to fumble for his keys. "That's not happening twice." Maybe Finn could manage one or two if he went slowly.

A low growl greeted him when he opened the door. The art book lay abandoned on the table.

"You'd best bloody well come out of there!" Finn yelled from the kitchen.

Diego froze in the doorway and then realized he must have been speaking to someone else.

"Finn! Who's in there?"

His pulse in his throat, he raced in and stopped, speechless. Finn stood alone in the kitchen, glowering at the answering machine, threatening it with the wooden meat tenderizer in his upraised fist.

"I don't know how he's done it," he turned his head. "But your nasty erstwhile lover has spelled himself inside your little box here and I've been unable to dislodge him. You didn't tell me he's a sorcerer."

Mitch. The answering machine. Mitch had left a message.

"He's not in the box," Diego explained, while he pried Finn's fingers from his improvised club. "It's just his voice."

"The boy can cast his voice? Into far away objects? By your expression, this news is meant to reassure me. I am by no means reassured."

Telephones took some explaining, but Finn finally dismissed the device with a disgusted snort as 'simply another machine'.

With a slow, painful breath, Diego pushed the play button.

"Diego… it's me. Look, I'm… I just wanted…"

Why did that voice still send a jolt through him? Why was he even listening to this?

"I saw what was in the apartment. I overreacted. I didn't mean those things. Hell, I don't know what I mean some days."

Mitch sounded tired, out of reserves. It was a familiar pattern, Mitch losing his temper and going away to brood, only to return to him later depressed and exhausted. And Diego was always the one who apologized.

"I thought we could meet for lunch. To talk. Like you wanted to. I'd be lying if I said I didn't miss you. It could work. It still could. I just need you to work on a couple things for me and everything would be perfect. Shit, Diego..."

Tears filled the disembodied voice. Diego squeezed his eyes shut and leaned his head against the wall. Mitch stretched out, cat-lazy and naked on the bed. Opening his arms and taking Diego in a hard embrace. That beautiful body dusted with fine, golden hair.

"Call me, love. Please."

Diego scrubbed a hand over his face, the other poised over the phone.

"You'll go to him?" Finn's voice yanked him into the present. He leaned against the counter, arms crossed over his chest.

"I don't know yet. This isn't really any of your business, you know." Even as he said it, he felt petty and ridiculous.

Finn shrugged. "Perhaps not. But did you listen to what he said? Truly listen? He wants you to crawl to him and make concessions. He gives you no promises, but expects you to make them. Some men long for another who will control them. Are you one of those?"

No. Yes. Sometimes.

"We have groceries to bring in. You feel up to giving me a hand?"

"His new lover has probably tossed him over the fence and that's why…"

"Let it go, Finn. If you're trying to help, it's not helping."

"Fair enough."

He brought up the shoes and the bag of clothes first so Finn wouldn't go out to the car in nothing but the pajama pants he'd taken to wearing around the apartment. Finn picked through the clothes and pulled on a pair of tight black jeans and a chamois shirt of deep burgundy which Diego had to help him button. The transformation astonished him, from half-wild asylum escapee to brooding bohemian.

I could just about take him out to dinner...

He squashed the thought as he watched Finn struggling to shove his feet into the sneakers without socks and without untying the laces.

"Here, wait, you'll hurt your poor feet." Diego knelt by him and took the right foot in his lap. The burns had faded to seashell pink. He ran a thumb over a line crossing Finn's instep. "How do they feel?"

"Quite comfortable at the moment," Finn answered, a soft husk to his voice.

Diego cleared his throat and shoved on the tube socks. He showed Finn how to open up the laces, and then had to demonstrate how to tie them.

"Bloody nuisance," Finn muttered, as he

stood rocking from heel to toe, staring morosely at his feet.

"Better than stepping on a stray piece of glass, or worse."

At the car, Finn hefted one of the bottles easily enough but Diego passed him on the stairs once, twice, and then a third time when Finn collapsed on the top step, his breaths reduced to short, desperate wheezes.

"And I thought I was out of shape." Diego crouched by him and nudged his arm. Finn's constricted breathing took on a whistling note, and Diego feared his asthma attack might deteriorate into a panic attack. "Hey, easy…"

Finn waved a hand, curling the fingers inward from little finger to index as if to snap further discussion off in his fist. Diego helped him back inside to the sofa, put the perishables away and wrestled the bottles into the bathroom.

"Do you want some of this heated?"

"Just as it is will be fine, simply—" Finn

called back from the sofa, before a fit of coughing stopped him.

Strange man. Diego would have preferred to put him in a hot bath but it only took four bottles to fill the tub. He had plenty in reserve to boil if necessary.

Shedding his clothes as he came, Finn staggered to the bathroom. He sank into the water in a boneless heap, his hair a thundercloud halo around his head when he submerged completely.

Diego watched from the doorway with anxious visions of 911 calls and ambulance crews assailing him. After a moment, though, Finn resurfaced and flashed that disarming, Cheshire Cat grin.

"No need to hover. I promise I won't drown. Or did you want to join me?"

"Too cold for me," Diego mumbled as he retreated, his hand shaking on the doorknob and an undeniable warmth spreading from his groin.

He paused by the phone, picked it up, and went to his desk. His fingers dialed Mitch's cell before he could stop them. Heart speeding, he disconnected. Dialed again. Hung up after half a ring.

"Dammit."

After staring at the phone as if it might bite him, he called his agent instead.

"Miriam? It's Diego. How are we doing?"

"Hey, sweetie! Not bad, not bad. Slow going but I've had a nibble or two."

"Nothing, huh?"

A gusty exhalation told him Miriam had plopped down in her chair. "I did warn you, hon. Market's flooded with dragon books. No one wants to look at one right now."

"But not from the dragon's POV. You even said—"

"I know, I know. And I love your work

and you know I believe in you. But we'd have a better chance if you had something else to hang your hat on first. Write me something really new and different. Something that'll catch their greedy little eyes and make dollar signs dance around their heads. Then when we have a contract and their attention, your dragon'll get a hearing."

"Right." Diego slumped in his chair. His blank computer screen glared at him. Soft splashes reached him from the bathroom. At least someone was enjoying himself.

"You are working, Diego. Tell me you are."

"I'm... things have been bad lately. I've been busy and... it's..."

"What's that man of yours done to you now?"

"Nothing." Diego swallowed hard, the hollow chasm threatening again. "He's left me."

"Oh, sweetie, damn. I'm sorry." Miriam's

voice softened for an instant before returning to brisk and forceful. "You're better off without that jerk anyway. Go out and find yourself some luscious hottie. Have him screw your brains out and clear your head."

Diego let out a sharp bark of laughter. "You know you ruin the whole maternal thing when you say things like that."

"Sure. But I made you laugh. Seriously, I think you need to get away for a little. Get out of the city, away from all the distractions and the reminders. The offer still stands."

"I'm a city boy. How would I survive in some cabin in Moosejaw?"

"New Brunswick, hon. Big difference. There's plumbing and power. It's not like you'd be roughing it up there. I even had a dish put up last summer, so you'd still be connected and everything. Tell me you'll think about it."

"I'll think about it." Diego leaned back in his chair and frowned at the bathroom door. The splashes had become constant, as if Finn were trying to swim in the tub. "I better go, Miriam."

Diego strode across to the bathroom and cringed at the slosh of water on the tiles. More tired than angry, he stuck his head around the door.

"Finn, do you think you could—"

He expected the small pools on the floor, not much of a shock. But the head poking up over the tub's rim stopped him cold. Round and covered in sleek, black fur, much smaller than human, the head ducked and reappeared. Two white-less eyes peered at him, long whiskers twitched. Rat? Dog? Otter.

He slammed the door and collapsed against the wall in the hallway. The damned hallucinations were starting already.

"Finn!"

A rush of falling water, light, hurried footsteps and Finn knelt beside him, rivulets cascading from his hair. "What ails you? Have you fallen ill?"

"I'm… I think I'm starting a seizure."

"Hush, now." Finn took Diego's head between his hands, long thumbs stroking his cheeks. "You aren't."

Diego gazed into those black eyes, so close, so sure, and nearly believed him. "No, I am. I'm seeing things."

"Things?"

"I saw a… an animal in the tub instead of you."

Finn's forehead crinkled. "You're a hard man to be angry with, but this has gone from amusing to three hairs short of infuriating."

He seized Diego by the upper arms and stood, lifting him to eye level. Diego's feet dangled above the floor. "All the time I've spent hiding what I am and when I finally come out in the open to someone, he refuses to believe me."

"Please put me down," Diego whispered. "I'll hurt us both when I seize."

"You will not fall into a fit. I would feel it. The lightning sparks in your head well beforehand." Finn carried him down the hall, set him on the sofa, and pressed him back against the cushions. "Be still now. Watch."

Diego couldn't have torn his eyes away if his life depended on it. Finn stood before him, arms spread, full erection jutting I-beam straight from the tops of his thighs.

God, he's beautiful. Even with all his ribs showing.

A soft prickling ran up Diego's arms like ants with static-electric feet. For an instant, Finn's skin glowed a soft blue white, and then he melted, his long body collapsing in on itself. His hair shortened and spread into black fur over his skin. The otter stood where Finn should have been. Another melting and an ebony crane replaced the otter. The crane clacked its beak and shifted to cormorant. Wolf, bear and coal-black stallion followed in lightning succession.

Diego's head throbbed. An odd whimper came from far away, though the vibration in his throat indicated he was the source.

The horse stamped a hoof, shook his mane, and melted into a huge, longhaired tomcat, its bushy tail twitching like an aggravated train signal.

"Well, my hero?" The cat spoke quite clearly in Finn's voice. "Are you convinced? Or do I shift to sea dragon?"

The gift of speech refused to return. Diego could only stare open-mouthed. The cat padded over and leaped onto the sofa beside Diego to rub up against him, purring. Then it sat up on its haunches and changed again, expanding until Finn sat there.

"Diego?"

He shook his head, gasped for air when he finally recalled how to breathe, and buried his head in his hands. Hallucinations. Dreams. He'd been asleep since the day Mitch left. Finn was merely a product of his heartsick imagination. Usually his dreams weren't so crisp and clear, though, and Tia Carmen had met him. Perhaps she was an illusion as well. It all was.

"And even the dreams are dreams," he whispered as the couch lurched under him.

"Enough, enough," Finn murmured and slid a hand under Diego's chin to lift his head.

He stroked his fingers back through Diego's close-cropped hair and closed the distance between them. The touch of his lips sent a hard jolt from Diego's heart to his sac, so soft, so gentle and yet insistent, full of heated promise. For a moment, he yielded, his lips moving in answer, aching to surrender to the need he felt in both of them.

This is wrong. So wrong.

"Finn..." he whispered against those sensual lips, and managed to pull back. "Why did you do that?"

Finn's eyes searched his face. "You

needed me to. Didn't you?"

"I don't think… I mean, we don't even know each other…"

"Diego." Finn's smile became uncertain. "You've given me shelter. Fed me. Slept with me in your arms. Can you still call us strangers?"

"But it's not right… to… to take advantage of you. In your situation. In mine." Damn. This was coming out all wrong. "I'm a huge mess. I'm no good for anyone. Especially not right now. I'd just be using you because I hurt like hell."

"And this is wrong?"

"Yes! Dammit, yes, it's wrong! I can't just sleep with you because you're convenient." *And you're not even human.*

Finn drew back, eyes burning. For a moment, Diego feared he would start a shouting match. Instead, he shook his head and stumbled off to his room.

Diego wrapped his arms hard around himself, waiting for the seizure that never came. If it was all a dream, he still had to live in it. As long as he existed here, he had to accept the peculiar rules and realities handed to him. He couldn't even say why he resisted so stubbornly. Throughout his childhood, he had wished so fervently for some hint of magic in the world he thought his heart would break. Now the evidence stood before him, a being who defied the laws of conventional physics, and he did all he could to reject the miracle.

Not to mention hurt the miracle's feelings.

His legs still trembled but he rose and found Finn kneeling at the window, arms on the sill. He'd pulled the pajama bottoms back on, darker stripes decorating the black cotton where his hair had dripped. Diego leaned in the doorway, searching for the right thing to say.

"Is it all like this?" Finn whispered.

"These machine-plagued, overcrowded places? Dead boxes of steel and stone. The poisoned air. Is it all in ruins?"

He sounded so broken, so sick with grief, Diego's confusion and misery evaporated. "There are wild places left. Beautiful places." *Probably even in Ireland.*

"Are there? I wish I could see them…"

"You could fly away," Diego suggested softly. "If I showed you on a map, could you find a place?"

Finn wiped his eyes, his laugh edging toward hysterical. "But that's just what I tried to do. To fly away. I'm so weak. Every small effort exhausts me. I fell out of the sky. And crawled back to you."

"I don't understand. If you can't even leave the city, how did you cross the ocean? Did you swim?"

"Not a bit of it. Saltwater doesn't agree with me. I… what's the expression? I stowed away."

Diego considered this as he fetched a towel and knelt behind Finn to dry his hair. "Wasn't the ship made mostly of steel?"

Finn shrugged. "Yes. If I were something small, a mouse perhaps, I thought I could hide among the wooden crates and do well enough. So much iron bearing down around me, day after day, crushing, stifling, choking the life spark from me." He trailed off, fists clenched, breath shuddering. "Mother of waters, it was an idiotic thing to do. I don't know how I survived, or why I tried so hard to after the first week. But I was desperate."

"Desperate? Why?"

To Diego's chagrin, Finn buried his face in his hands, his long frame wracked by sobs.

"Please… oh, don't do that…"

"I'm lost," Finn wailed. "Exiled in this cursed, blighted world." He whirled about to hide his face against Diego's shoulder.

With a queasy feeling of borrowing trouble, Diego wrapped his arms tight around him and held on until the earthquake of sobs subsided.

"Now." Diego tried to sound stern while stroking his back. "You've been ducking the question for days. What the hell happened when you came back to the world?"

Rather than answer, Finn pulled him down to lie beside him on the air mattress and settled his head on Diego's chest. The physical contact seemed to calm him and his voice held steady when he spoke again.

"I woke to a draining feeling, as if the life bled from me. It was day, but something blocked the sunlight. Surfacing brought me through a layer of reeking black spread on the water's surface. In my sleep, I had drifted to the river's mouth, near the sea. Gulls and fish floundered in this inky horror, which clung to everything. I tried to save the ones I could reach but most were already dead, and I felt as if I were dying as well. A huge ship hove into sight, a long pipe hung from its side sucking up the black muck with no regard for what lay in its path. Gods only know how, but I gained the shore.

"By shifting smaller and smaller, I managed to roll in the sand to rid myself of most of the reeking mess. But I was terribly ill and lay there in the refuse and the reeds until the sun set. When I could move again, I tried the Veil. But the passage was closed, the human world cut off from Fairy. I called and called through the night but no one came. No one. Not even someone come to gloat.

"They are gone. I am all that is left."

The theory, at least, was familiar to Diego. Celtic legends held numerous descriptions of the thin line between the world of humans and magical beings, which in the age of heroes seemed to have been permeable and easy to cross.

"Maybe they just changed the rules," he ventured. "While you slept."

"Perhaps." Finn flung an arm around his waist and drew him closer. "There were those in the court who wanted to remove the passage entirely ever since the last retreat of the ice when it became clear humans would thrive and multiply. The Veil has become less and less… accessible over the centuries."

"Hold on." Diego stilled his hand, realizing he'd been combing his fingers through Finn's hair. "Are you saying you've been around since the last Ice Age?"

Finn lifted his head and kissed Diego's jaw. "Of course I have. You have as well, my hero, though I know you don't recall now."

No, he couldn't be saying… Diego dismissed that line of thinking, able to deal with only so much in one afternoon.

"But someone should have come. To

close the boundary and leave one of the Folk stranded... unthinkable. But perhaps they were forced. Or thought me dead. I don't know." Finn heaved a shaky breath.

"So you got to shore and then what happened?" Diego prompted, to distract him.

"The fishermen's huts were gone, replaced by huge blocks of steel and glass. Some of these spewed noxious vapors. I was stranded in a purely human world where, unchecked, the human tendencies to conquer and control had run rampant. Two choices, I told myself—lie down and die, or find out if truly all lay in ruins. I wasn't ready to die. And unlike some, I have never held that humans are all senseless, evil savages."

"Um, thanks for that."

"You are more than welcome."

Finn's hand wandered down to Diego's hip. He grabbed it and pulled it back up to his chest.

"I became a dog. One of the best ways to hide in a human settlement. Out in the open. There was a village, of sorts, nearby. Too big for my liking. Too many people and strange machines. But I did learn that humans no longer believe in the Fair Folk. Stories for children, that's what we've become. The reverence and fear and even love we had once received from humans reduced to ridiculous caricatures of little men in buckled shoes." Finn snorted in disgust. "Leprechauns."

"Ah. Sorry about that."

"How were you to know?" Finn stroked circles around one of Diego's shirt buttons. "I reasoned Eire had become so overrun with humans because it is so small. I could, after all, fly from Ulster to the southernmost tip of Munster in a day. America was rumored to be vast, I recalled. Endless expanses of woods, mountains so tall their heads pierced the clouds. There I would find clean water again and perhaps others who had been left behind. Imagine my horror when I left the ship and found..." He waved a hand toward the window. "This."

"You were right, though. It isn't all like this..." Diego trailed off when he realized Finn was unbuttoning his shirt. "Please don't do that."

Finn ignored him and tugged the shirttails from his jeans. The hand stroking his stomach felt so damn good. So easy, just to give in. His breath caught when Finn shifted his head to take a nipple in his mouth in a hard-suctioned kiss.

"Holy mother of... oh, shit..." Diego whispered.

"An odd deity to pray to, but who am I to dictate such things?" Finn smiled against his skin, his hand sliding under Diego's waistband.

"Stop that! I said no!" Diego hauled the hand back out though his member pressed achingly hard against his jeans. He tried to sit up but Finn moved so fast to straddle him, he had no time to do more than cry out in shock. Pinned, both wrists trapped above his head in Finn's frighteningly strong grip, he struggled and snarled in helpless frustration.

"Let me go!"

Finn shook his head, curling forward to kiss his eyelids. "Your scent calls to me. You want this. You need me to take you. I need this."

"Dammit, Finn, I'm not an animal." Diego stopped struggling and caught Finn's gaze. It wasn't a trick of the light. His eyes actually glowed red when emotions ran high. "Yes, my body wants sex. I can't help that. I'm hurting and lonely, and it's a natural physical reaction to you being nearby. But I'm not ready. And I wouldn't be doing it for the right reasons. I'd feel awful afterward. Guilty and ashamed and… I just can't do this right now. Please. Can you understand that?"

A low growl rumbled in Finn's chest, but

he cut it short and dismounted to turn back to the window. "Forgive me. You've been nothing but kind to me. I wished only to help you. You carry such a terrible ball of pain under your heart. And you will not let the tears flow to release the poison. It's no wonder you fall into fits. But you let no one help you. As if you believe you deserve the agony."

Diego wanted to protest. What a thing to say. But he couldn't recall a single tear since Mitch left him. Not that he hadn't felt like sobbing. Why hadn't he cried? Why couldn't he?

"It's all right," he murmured. "I appreciate the thought."

"Please, let me help you…"

This wouldn't do. Finn was close to tears himself again.

"Look, if you really want to help, go clean up that mess in the bathroom. I don't mind if you keep your water in there a couple of days. But it doesn't belong on the floor."

Finn stared at him, blinking. "Oh. Very well. I didn't realize." He rose and returned to the bathroom.

"Don't you want a mop or some..." Diego followed and trailed off when he reached the doorway. One hand stretched out toward the floor, palm down, Finn watched calmly as the water flowed back up into the tub.

"Never mind."

He went to the kitchen to start dinner, needing some space to breathe and to think.

Chapter 6: Art and Asthma

At dinner, Finn recovered his usual humor and inquisitiveness, as if nothing had happened in the bedroom. He declared Diego's chicken 'quite edible' though he mourned Tia Carmen's absence. Halfway through eating, he leaped up to retrieve the art book from the living room. Nothing would satisfy him until Diego slid his chair closer to explain each picture.

Luckily there were captions. Diego hadn't studied art since college. He recalled enough to relate a bit about the major artists' lives, though, which interested Finn more than technique or theory.

"But why?" Finn asked, after Diego explained Michelangelo's struggle with the Sistine Chapel.

"Why what? Why did he keep going, or why the ceiling?"

Finn shook his head. "No, no. Why any

of it? Why do humans insist on making these representations of other things?"

That stumped Diego. "Don't you find them beautiful?"

"Some of them, surely. Is it because you destroy so much beauty that you are compelled to create it?"

"I…" Diego drummed his fingers on the table, trying to construct a solid, honest answer. "I think people have asked that question for as long as we could draw. And you'd probably get as many answers as there are artists."

Finn snickered. "Is this what you meant by 'ducking the question'?"

"Yes." Diego smiled, the tight band around his heart easing. "I'm not an artist or an art historian, so I'm probably not qualified to answer your question. I mean, some art's symbolic, or satirical, or provocative instead of beautiful. I think maybe it's something about helping the viewer see things in a different way.

In a way you hadn't thought of before. Art evokes an emotional response. Maybe not the one the artist intended. But some kind of gut reaction."

Finn traced over the lines of David's marble face. "I don't understand. The words, yes, but I can't grasp it."

"Like holding water in your hand."

"No, that I can do." Finn cocked his head to the side. "Ah. You jest. I wasn't certain you knew how."

"I'm a little out of practice." Diego finished his beer and started to clear the table. "Maybe we should go see some in person. Art, that is. It's hard to feel the real impact from pictures in a book."

Finn's head rested on his arms, his eyelids sliding shut. "I don't think I would survive a trip to Italy."

"We don't have to go that far." Explanations could wait until morning, or the next afternoon, or whenever Finn could manage the stairs better.

After he put Finn to bed, Diego realized he'd never called social services about placement for him. "Don't suppose they have a Fairy Support Division anyway," he muttered to his computer. "I can't believe I just said that."

* * * *

Finn turned the corner into yet another room and sighed. More blasted odd things on the walls he couldn't fathom. In the crush of humans, he had lost Diego many rooms before. A large group had come between them, all tagging behind and hanging on the words of a strident-voiced woman who pointed at the things on the walls and said incomprehensible things about them. When he had extricated himself from the herd, Diego was nowhere to be seen. His absence was like standing on a cliff in a hurricane. Nothing to lean against. No shelter to be seen.

They had stood in a grand hall at one point, one with lovely, ceiling-high windows looking out on trees and with interesting representations of naked or near-naked humans every few feet. Diego had waved a hand to the chairs by the wall and told him the name of the room. "Come back here if we get separated or if you get tired. Just sit down and wait for me. No one will bother you if you don't touch the statues."

"European Sculpture Court," Finn repeated under his breath. He knew he wasn't anywhere near the place. Diego had also said to ask one of the people in the jackets with the shiny buttons to help him if he became lost. But they all looked so forbidding and stern, he'd been rather anxious about approaching any of them. The last person he'd talked to in a jacket with shiny buttons had locked him in an iron cage.

Lovely buttons, though. Made his fingers itch to touch.

He sat down on a stone bench in front of a man-high, painted canvas. As a representation of something, it made no sense, but the colors shone bold and bright. Not for the first time that day, he wished he could decipher the lines and circles humans used to label everything. Perhaps it held a clue as to what he was supposed to see.

A small boy flopped down beside him, legs swinging.

"Are you tired, too?"

The boy glanced sideways at him with a frown. *Gods of night, the children here are all so suspicious.* For a moment, he thought the boy might run away.

"I guess." The boy shrugged.

"Don't you like this place?"

"It's OK. I like the armor and swords and stuff. The rest is boring." He peered at Finn more closely. "You talk funny."

"I'm from far away."

"No, I mean like you can't breathe right."

Finn rubbed at his chest and coughed. Observant child. "It, ah, gives me trouble sometimes."

The boy nodded. "I have asthma, too. You probably forgot your inhaler, didn't you? My mom yells at me when I forget mine."

"Yes, exactly." Whatever an inhaler was, it sounded plausible.

A portly man sat down beside the boy. The set of his features indicated annoyance; the tone of his voice confirmed it. "You're not even looking at anything, Jaime. I don't know why we bother coming."

"I'm tired," the boy muttered. "And thirsty."

"At least look at some of it. Read the plaques. Jasper Johns is a very important artist, the father of pop art…"

The man droned on and on in a pompous, self-important way. No wonder the boy was so bored. If Diego had described art to him that way, he would have dropped off to sleep.

Finn nudged the boy's elbow and whispered. "Do you feel anything when you look at it? My friend says art is supposed to make you feel things. Or see things differently. Or something of that sort."

The father halted his exposition in surprise. The boy glanced up at Finn and then at the painting. "I like the colors."

"As do I." Finn nodded. He cocked his head to one side, to see the blobs of red, blue and yellow from a different angle. "I think," he said, a smile creeping onto his face, "that I might begin to understand. There is a playfulness to this one. I think it must have been great fun to paint."

"Like the colors made the artist happy?"

Jaime leaned forward on the bench.

"Perhaps so."

The boy wandered closer to examine the painting in detail while his father turned to Finn and stared. "You're good. I can't get him to look at the paintings to save my life."

"One hopes it wouldn't come to that," Finn answered, his brow wrinkling in concern.

The man laughed as if he'd made a joke. "First time in America? You're Irish, aren't you?"

"Yes." He considered a moment. The man seemed friendly enough now. "I don't suppose you could point the way to the European Sculpture Court? I'm just a wee bit lost."

The man pulled out a rectangle of paper and Finn watched in fascination as he unfolded it to a much larger rectangle. A map. Ah. Not that it did him much good. Maps confused him as much as writing. But he listened as the man described the way back, which sounded easy enough. He thanked him and started off, confident he would find his way.

Several flights of stairs and what seemed several miles later, he still wandered. His chest hurt. Lungs could be such a bother. He'd considered shifting to fish and plunging into one of the fountains he passed but the water smelled worse than the stuff from Diego's sink.

This is ridiculous. Lost in a bizarre labyrinth, unable to find Diego because of the confusion of human scents, he bristled. Was he or was he not Fionnachd the Hunter? The one who had tracked the red-eared boar through endless thickets and mazes of thorns for the Queen's pleasure?

"Long ago, bucko, in a different world," he muttered, and leaned against a doorway to catch what was left of his breath. Not to mention the fact that no one had ever called him Fionnachd the Hunter except Herself, and only that once. And the boar had been so frightened he'd let the poor thing go.

"Are you all right, sir?"

Finn glanced down and forced a smile. One of the shiny-buttoned ones had asked the question. Lovely thing. Chestnut skin. Hair plaited into a hundred tiny braids like rushes decorating her head.

"Yes, beautiful lady, I'm quite well." The lie was ruined by the wheeze in his voice.

"Mmhm. Right."

"Forgot my inhaler."

"Oh, hon, you should know better at your age." The woman's voice had shifted from professional to maternal scolding. "We better get you to sit down. You here with someone?"

"European Sculpture Court... supposed to meet him there..." Why did his chest constrict further the harder he tried to breathe?

"All right, baby, all right. It's just through there. Come on." The woman took his elbow, not to restrain him, he realized, but to hold him up. He gave her a wan smile. Such a confident little thing. She might be able to catch him if he toppled at that.

Under the final archway, relief flooded through him to see the long-sought hall. Better still, Diego stood in the center of the room, eyes searching the crowd. Finn's mouth twitched up into a foolish grin. Compact and lean, those oh-too-serious features, those heart-melting eyes, Diego was a beautiful sight.

"That's him," Finn murmured to his guide and pointed.

She chuckled. "Oh, you got it bad, boy."

"What do I have?"

"For him. Well, not that I blame you. He's damn cute."

Nonsense. He wasn't lovesick for any human. Never again. Diego was lovely and it would have been wonderful to seduce him. He was certainly grateful for all the man had done, could even call him a friend, but he wasn't becoming attached to him.

Diego spotted them while the woman helped Finn into a chair. The profound relief in those loam-dark eyes, the way he hurried over as if Finn were the most important thing in the universe—

Oh, blast. Perhaps the pretty woman was right. He wasn't so naïve that he didn't recognize the signs of rescuer infatuation. The warmth of it had spread through him when Diego's gentle hands had caressed the filth from him under the little waterfall in the bathroom.

But by now, gods help him, it was more than that.

"Everything all right?" Diego glanced between him and the woman.

"He says he forgot his inhaler."

For an eye-blink, Diego stared. Then he threw up his hands in a credible show of exasperation. "*Ay, dios!* How many times do we have to go through this?"

Good man. Finn hung his head in his best imitation of remorse. "I'm sorry." He fought to hold off the impending coughing fit until the woman went away. The last thing he wanted to hear again was the word 'doctor'.

"You boys aren't going to make me call in a medical emergency, are you? I hate all the damn paperwork."

Diego put a hand on Finn's shoulder. "No, ma'am. He just needs to rest and then I'll get him home."

As soon as she walked out of earshot, Finn doubled over his knees to muffle the barking coughs that threatened to shred his lungs. Diego sat down beside him to rub his back.

"This was a stupid idea. I'm sorry. You just looked so much better this morning."

Finn closed his fist on the air to cut off Diego's self-flagellation. "I'll live. Don't fret."

"I don't think I want to take you back on the subway, though, when you can barely walk." Diego was silent for a moment. "Could you shift to something smaller? Not here in front of everyone. But something I could carry. Like a mouse?"

Finn leaned back in the chair. "It takes a good deal more effort... to become something so much smaller. The excess mass... has to go somewhere, you know."

"No, I didn't. I suppose I never gave the mechanics of magic much thought." Diego chewed his bottom lip in that endearing expression he had when he thought hard. "How much smaller could you become? Without too much effort?"

"Oh, say, a terrier-sized dog. A weasel, perhaps."

Diego nodded and patted his knee. "Wait here a sec."

The sight of that shapely backside

walking away was almost enough to distract him from the pain. A thousand and three ways to conquer Diego's reluctance had crossed his mind. His concern, his empathy, his need to help those in pain all made him an absurdly easy mark, but the thought left a sour taste. He wanted Diego willing and aching for him, not out of a sense of obligation or pity.

On the other hand, hang it all, I haven't had sex in seven hundred years.

It didn't help that the pedestal directly in front of him held a statue of a faun cavorting with a woman, her luscious body pressed between his furry thighs. He closed his eyes and thought hard about frozen lakes. With a freezing rain falling. And his balls trapped in the ice. That did it.

He pulled a second chair close and curled up across them to wait.

* * * *

Diego hurried back with the shopping bag he'd wheedled out of the girl behind the gift shop counter. His pulse lurched when he spotted Finn, apparently asleep or passed out.

"Oh, gawd, there's bag people even in here?" a nasal female voice whined on his left.

Diego risked a glance over at the trio of young women who had stopped to stare at Finn.

The one with streaked hair giggled. "He looks more like a refugee from Fashion Week."

"Homeless designers, right? Like, ohmigod, you can't live in that box. It's not Perrier!" They collapsed against each other in gales of laughter.

"Excuse me." Diego made a point of walking through them to Finn and shook his shoulder gently. "Time to wake up. I know you don't feel well so let's get you home."

Finn blinked, his look seeming to ask why he was saying such idiotically obvious things. But with a glance at the girls and back at Diego, his expression hardened.

When Finn sat up and the girls began to walk off, a chair leaped out of line directly into one girl's shin. She stumbled into the others and they all tumbled in a heap of shrieks and flailing limbs. Finn's grim smile told Diego all he needed to know.

"That wasn't very nice." He took Finn's arm to help him up.

"They're nasty little bits. And they were upsetting you."

"Still, you can't go around..." Diego shook his head and led him off to the nearest bathroom. "If I'm really upset, I'll take care of it myself, okay? Please don't think you have to fight my battles for me."

Finn fell silent except for his wheezing. Offended, Diego thought. A check to make certain the bathroom was empty, and he pulled Finn into the handicapped stall. He helped Finn out of his clothes, praying for a moment's privacy. Two sets of feet visible under the door, one shod and the other bare, would look bad.

"Can you manage?" he whispered as he folded Finn's clothes into a neat bundle and shoved them into the bag with the sneakers on the bottom.

Finn heaved a hitching breath, closed his eyes, and melted. Diego looked down; a black ferret lay on the tiles at his feet.

"Don't ask me to get up. I can't," the ferret muttered in Finn's voice.

A twinge of anxiety fluttered in Diego's stomach. Ferrets tended to be nippy. "Please don't bite me."

The absence of any smart-ass rejoinders to this told him how bad off Finn was. He gathered the soft-furred body up in both hands and eased him into the bag atop the clothes. "I'll try not to jostle you too much."

The ferret grunted and curled into a ball,

his head vanishing under his body.

All the way home, an itch lodged between Diego's shoulders. An unreasoning fear gripped him that some over-zealous security guard would call out, 'Hold up, sir. Let's see what's in the bag.' Not that transporting ferrets was illegal but he'd have to concoct some explanation about not wanting to leave his pet at home. Lying convincingly wasn't one of his strong suits. He breathed easier when he closed the apartment door.

Finn lay limp and unmoving when he lifted him out. He gathered the furred body close to his chest. "I'm so sorry."

"Not that I want to discourage your embraces," Ferret-Finn whispered. "But could you put me in the bath?"

Diego slid him into the water and held him, fingers tingling, until he shifted into a fish. Bass, grouper, trout, he had no idea what sort but one that looked comfortable lounging in a bath at any rate.

He'd banished the thought of handing Finn over to any agency, certain he would end up in some formaldehyde tank in Area 51, after being thoroughly interrogated, sampled, tormented and dissected, of course.

Later, when he settled Finn on the sofa with his bottled water and bananas, a plan began to percolate. He showed Finn how to operate the TV remote with cautionary statements about how little of what the picture box showed was real.

"Like a play?"

"Yes, exactly like." Diego thanked the heavens that he understood the concept of drama. "I'm going out for a bit. Please don't go anywhere."

Finn nodded in a distracted way, his head cocked to one side as he watched Teletubbies bouncing across the screen.

Diego went first to deliver his articles

due at various local magazines, then called Miriam to see if she had a few minutes for him and left a message on Mitch's voicemail.

"I'll be at Café Lucca by two. Should be there for about an hour if you still want to talk."

He had to stop on a bench when he closed the phone, his heart slammed so hard against his breastbone. *Why did I do that? I'm too keyed up to see him today.*

But to call Mitch back and cancel would make him look ridiculous. What was he hoping for, though? Reconciliation? An apology? One of those scenes where he could say the things he longed to and feel vindicated?

A black pigeon landed on the bench next to him, startling him out of his ruminations. "Finn?"

The pigeon paid no attention to him, pecked at a few crumbs, and fluttered away. He supposed it was asking too much to expect a regular pigeon to answer him.

* * * *

The view from Miriam's office, perched high above Fifth Avenue, always made him dizzy. She moved the chair around to face the inside wall for him.

"What's up, kiddo? You have something brilliant to tell me?" Miriam's chair squealed in protest as she plopped back down, thick calves tucked back.

"No, sorry. It's more along the lines of a favor. About your cabin—"

"You changed your mind! Good boy."

"Well, no, it's not for me, exactly. It's for a friend."

Miriam sat back to another chorus of metallic squeaks. Her sharp gray eyes pinned him fast. "A friend."

"Yes, um." Diego lost the battle against squirming. "He's not doing well in the city. Has some respiratory issues. I think the air is slowly killing him."

"Is he hot?"

"Miriam, for God's sake."

She shrugged. "You are the most inhibited gay man I've ever met. I was just asking."

"But it's not relevant." Diego closed his eyes a moment. "I just wanted to know if you'd take him with you the next time you head up that way."

"Then his looks are relevant. It's a long drive. I'm not ferrying anyone, friend of yours or not, if he's ugly."

"He's not."

"So why don't you take him yourself?"

"My car would never make it."

"So we rent you one."

"I'll get lost."

"You call me if you do."

"And I don't want to leave the apartment

standing empty."

"Mrs Montoya will watch it for you."

"But I'd feel so out of place in the country."

"Just take your new hunk and go. Can't beat the privacy."

"What if I have a seizure?"

"You said they're under control."

"Yes, but—"

She held up both hands. "Fine, fine. If I meet him and like him, I'll drag him along. If he's a friend of yours, I'm sure he's a good enough guy. But I'm not going up there until June, just so you know." She leaned forward to peer at him. "Bit off more than you can chew with this one?"

"No. That is..." Diego slumped in his chair. "My head's not on straight. I know any decisions I make right now are suspect."

"You need to get over the last one, hon. What better way than someone new?"

"I can't do that to Finn. Treat him like some piece of therapeutic equipment." He twisted his scarf in his hands. "I might be seeing Mitch this afternoon."

"You know I love you, but you're an idiot."

"Yes, ma'am."

With Miriam's assurances that she would come over for dinner soon, Diego left for the Village. Café Lucca, nestled alongside Washington Square, had been their favorite meeting place at the start of his relationship with Mitch, a place to peoplewatch and sit with heads close together in earnest, whispered conversation. Happy memories. Now the inviting scents of coffee and pastry, the dark-wood table by the window, the comfortable, chatting couples, all made him feel as if he'd been sucked dry.

We are the hollow men.

What a time for his brain to start reciting

T S Elliot.

A hand fell on his shoulder, turned him. He caught a glimpse of pale blue eyes before strong arms wrapped around him. "Damn, it's good to see you."

Diego shivered and Mitch hugged him tighter, rubbing his back. So easy to surrender, to let himself believe again. He clung for a moment, breathing in Mitch's unmistakable mix of musk and cologne, a stab of desire threatening to take him out at the knees.

Pushed to his knees, Mitch's hands rough with passion. Fingers kneaded his shoulders with impatient force as he took his time with the trouser button and zipper. The hard moan from above when he wrapped his lips around Mitch's cock...

The memory jerked to a halt. Mitch had never reciprocated and fallen to his knees for him. Not once. Gone down on him a time or two in bed to coax him along when he didn't feel like sex, but never that gesture of helpless lust and adoration.

"It's good to see you, too." Diego pulled back and slid into a seat by the window. "I guess... I wanted to make sure you're okay. Your last message, it worried me."

Mitch laughed and flung himself into the chair beside him. "I was worried about you." He seized Diego's hand to kiss his knuckles. "You know how I worry."

"Yes." Diego stared at their joined hands, hit by an odd dislocation, everything distant and miniaturized. "Mitch, I..."

"Sh, don't apologize—"

I wasn't going to.

"I've been doing a lot of thinking. Here's the deal. I have a new place now, one of those converted lofts, very cool. Lots of space. Lots of light. Let's get you out of Brooklyn. Move in with me. There'll be less distractions for you. And if you want to do some charity work, fine. I understand. Help out at one of the shelters or something. Volunteer at the library. I don't mind. Just so long as it's not this maverick, unsupervised stuff you do now. That's where you get into trouble…"

The words reached Diego from far away, as if an old movie played in the next room with the sound turned low. Some part of him wanted to be angry. After all the harsh words, the agony Mitch had put him through, he thought he could waltz back in like this, as if nothing had happened?

Most of his attention, though, went to the wall he felt rising between them, a new course of stones added with every sentence Mitch spoke. Not the Great Wall, perhaps. Hadrian's Wall. About waist high.

He patted Mitch's arm, resisting the urge to stroke the fine, golden hairs. "Stop. Please. I can't. I can't move in with you. I can't start all this up again."

"Well, I suppose I could move back if you really can't leave the neighborhood." Mitch's brows drew together; the smile vanished.

"No, you're not listening. I love you. I probably always will." God help me. "But I can't be with you anymore, living with my stomach always in knots, waiting for the next time you blow up at me."

"Diego…"

"Christ, please don't cry. You know what that does to me and I need to get through this."

"But I need you, baby," Mitch whispered. "I'm no good on my own."

"You need someone; I'd say that's true. But I don't think you need me specifically." His chest ached, that ball of black pain Finn had described making itself known. "I had to see you, I think, to be sure how I feel. And now I know. I can't do it anymore."

"You've been upset. It's been hard on

you. I can see that. But I don't want you making hasty decisions…"

"This isn't hasty. And it hurts like hell. But I think it's the best thing for both of us."

"How can you say that? You'll never make it on your own. You can't even scrape up grocery money some weeks." Mitch's eyes narrowed, his voice dropping to an ugly snarl. "Or did you find someone else? That fast? After all that moaning about how you missed me, you had someone on the side all along?"

"Please don't get bitchy. Please. No, I don't have a new lover."

"So I can still see you?" The hand holding Diego's clutched harder.

"No. Not a good idea. And neither one of us is so naïve that we'd think we can 'still be friends'." Diego reached out to trace a finger along Mitch's jaw. "I'm sorry. I wish…"

Mitch moved suddenly, grabbed Diego by the back of the head, and yanked him into a fierce, bruising kiss. "Something to remember me by, sweetheart. On those long, lonely nights when you're jacking yourself off 'cause no one else will put up with you."

He stared in mortified silence as Mitch stalked out. Of all the…

Halfway back to the subway, he realized that for all Mitch's talk about reconciliation, he had never apologized. Not for a single thing.

* * * *

Diego trudged up the steps to his place, lead feet stumbling twice. Now he had to deal with whatever Finn had been up to in his absence. Four o'clock. He'd been out too long.

No Finn on the sofa. Too much to ask that he'd be napping. Bedroom and bath stood empty. He pushed open the swinging kitchen door and jerked to a halt with one foot across the threshold.

Stacked four feet high on the table, all of Diego's glassware winked in the light. Clear glass mixing bowls served as the base of this bizarre construct, topped by his red glass dinner plates. Tumblers and wine glasses rose from there in physically impossible positions, feet balanced precariously on rims, bowls stuck to neighboring ones with no visible support. The whole structure formed a lumpy, inverted pyramid, a temple to improbability.

Finn leaned against the counter, regarding his work with a thoughtful expression.

"What is all this?" Diego managed to choke out.

"'S art." Finn's words came out thick and slurred. "D'you like it?"

Diego scrubbed both hands over his face. "It's… interesting. Though I wish you wouldn't put my glassware in jeopardy. Is it held together by magic?"

"No. This stuff." Finn held out a tube of

all-purpose adhesive. "Saw a man on't picture box use it. Smells bloody awful." He swayed and slapped a hand on the counter to steady himself, mumbling something about the floor turning to liquid.

Sniffing glue. Wonderful.

"Diego…" Finn's eyes searched for him before they rolled back in his head. Diego flung himself across the room and caught him under the arms. Finn's head landed with a thump on his shoulder.

"My poor friend," he murmured. The thought crystallized, clear as the glass piled on his table. He had to take Finn out of the city himself. No one else would do.

Chapter 7: Taking the Boy Out of the City

Finn woke the next morning with a ferocious headache. He rocked back and forth, curled over his knees, whimpering and moaning. When Tia Carmen brought him tea, he subsided into a listless heap on his air mattress.

"*Qué hacía?*" she whispered to Diego, outside his room.

"He tried his hand at, ah, modern art yesterday. The glue made him sick." He led her to the kitchen to show her.

"*Ay, dios!*" Her hands flew up to cover her mouth. "Do you have anything left to drink out of?"

"I have plastic cups. And coffee mugs. I've decided to keep it. Rather pretty in a funky sort of way, don't you think?"

She walked around it once and nodded. "It is better than some things you see in the museums. But I think if you want to keep the rest of your things, we should get him something *más seguro*... safer to work with."

From the chest she kept stocked for visiting grandchildren, she brought up a full box of sixty-four crayons. "Paper I think you have, Santiago. Now don't leave him alone so long again."

After she left, Diego brought crayons and paper to Finn's bed. "Feeling better?"

"A mite." He opened one eye a crack. "Are you angry with me?"

"No, no. Just, in the future, please don't rearrange things without asking me first." He lifted a lock of hair out of Finn's eyes. "I brought you a present."

Finn turned onto one elbow, his pained expression turning to wonder when Diego opened the box of crayons. "Ooo, lovely. What are these?"

"Colored wax, mostly. But you can draw

with them." He took out the burnt sienna and demonstrated, sketching a few simple shapes. "Any color you might want."

"Thank you..." Finn's voice cracked.

"What is it?"

"You've been so very kind to me. I think I've brought you nothing but trouble."

"Sh, that's not true." Diego patted his shoulder. "I'll be staying home today. We have something to talk about. Later, when you feel better."

Meanwhile, he had phone calls to make. First, to Miriam.

"Excellent!" she enthused. "I knew you'd come around, kiddo. Now don't you worry. I'll arrange everything. You just sit back and wait for my phone call. When do you want to go?"

"I thought maybe on Thursday. So we're not driving in weekend traffic."

"Always thinking. Your passport's valid? And your friend's?"

Diego's heart stuttered. *Passports. God.* One needed those now to cross the border.

"You there, hon?"

"Yes, sorry." He rummaged in the drawer for his passport and checked the date. "Just making sure. Mine's good."

"And his?"

"Finn's from Ireland," Diego blurted out, to stall for time.

"Oh, he's all set, then. I'll call you back this afternoon."

Why hadn't he thought of that? Even before the tightening of border security, Finn would still have needed identification. A driver's license. Something. They asked for everyone's...

No, wait. They asked for every human's ID. A solution presented itself, if Finn would agree to it.

He placed the next call to his father in Miami. After his mother died, his father had moved back to Florida, where the bulk of his family lived and he no longer had to struggle with English.

"*Hola, Papi.*"

"*Diego! Cómo estás?*"

"Fine, fine," he continued in Spanish. If he spoke anything else, his father would pretend not to understand. "Papi, I wanted to tell you I would be away for a while. Up in Canada."

"Why would you go there? Isn't it cold?"

"My agent thinks it will be good for me. For my writing. To get out of the city."

"*Mijo*, don't you have a real job yet?"

"This is my real job. Please, I don't want to start this again."

"Then why not come down here? Where you have family and sunshine. Where we can make sure you have enough to eat."

"I get enough to eat. Please don't worry. I wanted to leave the number in case you or Analisa need to find me."

"You truly want me to tell your sister? She will call, whether she needs to or not."

Diego smiled. Yes, she would, to complain about her husband and to gossip about the cousins. "That's all right, Papi. I don't mind."

"Don't get eaten by bears."

He laughed and assured his father he wouldn't.

That had been nearly painless, unlike their conversations a few years ago when Diego had first come out to his family. His sister had been shocked but accepting. His father had ranted and cried and hounded him for months about getting help for his 'illness'. Eventually the hand-twisting and hair-tearing had given way to a 'don't ask, don't tell' policy. Papi didn't ask about his personal life, he didn't offer any details, and relations evened out to stilted but civil.

Father John at the Mission was next, to let him know he wouldn't be able to do his usual rounds for a while. "Go, Diego," Father John reassured him. "Someone else will look in on everyone and make sure the cold weather warnings get out. You need a rest."

The last phone call went to Mitch's voicemail. Cowardly, perhaps, to leave a message, though Diego wasn't sure he owed him even that much any longer. He simply couldn't stand the thought of Mitch thinking he had slunk away and gone into hiding.

Around noon, after three false starts on a new story, he got up to check on Finn. The pooka sprawled on his stomach, one foot idly waving in the air, the tip of his tongue protruding from the corner of his mouth. A dozen sheets of paper littered the floor around him, most with random scribbles that appeared to be experiments in crayon technique. The one he leaned over now in such intense concentration seemed a more structured effort, a mosaic of carefully interlocked, jagged shapes.

Finn finished the shape drawn in Mango Tango, placed the crayon with the growing pile he had already used and nearly stuck his nose inside the box to search for the next one. He pulled out Eggplant, turned it in the light, and nodded in satisfaction before he noticed Diego crouched beside him.

He held out the clipboard. "What do you think?"

Diego studied it, the same anxiety gripping him as when a four-year-old handed him a picture he couldn't decipher. He always guessed wrong, earning him that brain-addling, scornful look only the pre-school set could manage.

"It's... well...."

Finn sat up. "You don't like it?"

"What is it?"

"Colors. They all have such different flavors."

"You haven't been eating them, have

you?"

"No, you mistake my meaning. They all speak to me in different voices. It's all a jumble in the box. On the paper, they sing more distinctly."

Diego stared at him, certain he still suffered from the effects of the glue, then studied the paper again.

"Like Jasper Johns," Finn tried again.

Ah. It did bear some resemblance to *False Start* from the museum's special exhibit. Interesting that of all the artists Finn had seen that day, he would find an affinity with someone so modern.

"I do like it. It's lively. Exuberant. Very well done for someone who claims he doesn't understand art." Diego handed the picture back. "Finn, if I could get you to one of the wild places that are left, would you want to go? That is, even if it means spending more than twelve hours in a car? I know there's a lot of aluminum and fiberglass in cars now but still, all that steel in the frame—"

Finn interrupted by flinging his arms around Diego's neck. "Yes, yes, I would wish to go! Put me in iron shackles. Shut me in an iron box. I don't care one whit. If there will be wilderness at the journey's end, I will endure anything."

"There's just one thing."

"Besides being shut up in a hurtling, metal machine?"

"Easy there." Diego rubbed Finn's arms, trying to soothe his shaking. "Right. Besides that. You'd need certain papers to cross the border and we've no way to get them for you. Not legally, anyway. And I can't afford the illegal way."

"Ah. A letter of passage?"

"Yes, something like that. So I need to ask you to do something for me and I feel sort of ashamed asking it."

"What would you ask of me, my hero?" Finn sat back, a wary light in his eyes.

"Until we cross the border, would you consider being my dog?"

Finn blinked at him and then let out an amused snort. "Diego, you shouldn't fear to ask me such simple things. Save your worries for when you must have something truly difficult of me."

"Even if it means wearing a collar for me?"

Finn flashed him a wicked grin. "Even so."

* * * *

Diego groaned when his alarm sounded at four in the morning. It had all seemed like such a good idea—beat the rush hour traffic out of the metro area, leave enough time for stops and getting lost, and still arrive at the cabin before full dark. Now the shaky, stomach roiling sensation of forcing his body out of bed too early on a few minutes' sleep made him want to burrow back under the covers and forget the whole thing.

The truck, though, had been delivered the evening before. A Ridgeline, much larger than Diego was comfortable driving, but Miriam insisted he would need something built for bad roads. All the luggage waited in the front hall and, perhaps by this time, an overexcited pooka as well. The pastor who served as the property's part-time caretaker would be expecting them and Miriam would kill him if he backed out now.

He had just stuck a foot outside the covers when a sudden weight depressed the mattress. Hard-nailed paws landed on his bare chest. A long tongue licked his face until he thought he might drown.

"Up, slugabed! I heard the clock. Up!"

"Finn, please." He pushed away the wet nose nuzzling at his ear. "You might want to move your big paws if you want me to get out of bed."

"Your pardon."

Diego rolled up and switched on the light. A huge, black dog sat at the foot of his bed, tongue lolling in a canine grin. "Does it suit?" the dog asked, feathered tail wagging madly.

"You look like a German Shepherd had an affair with a wolf."

"Is this a bad thing?"

"You're a very handsome specimen." Diego patted his shoulder. Such soft, thick fur, he wanted to bury his face in it. "Give me a few minutes. I need coffee. And a shower."

Dog-Finn leaped from the bed. "Can I offer any assistance?"

Anyone else Diego would have told yes. You can start the coffee while I get cleaned up.

Or take the luggage down to the truck. With Finn, though, he could imagine a few dozen ways such simple things might become disasters of titanic proportions.

"No, thank you. Relax for a few minutes. Grab yourself some breakfast."

"My stomach's too full of flutters."

So instead, Finn danced around him, getting underfoot while he tried to get ready. The head-butt against his knees while he shaved hit the limit of his endurance.

"Go find your collar, please," he suggested to gain a few moments' peace.

Finn loped off and returned with the nylon and plastic collar between his teeth.

"Sh, you'll wake Tia Carmen." Diego pointed to the tail thudding against the hardwood.

Unintelligible mumbles issued from around the collar. The tail stopped but the tags jangled when Finn shook his head. One tag had been purchased at a pet store and engraved 'Finn—please return to Diego Sandoval' with his cell number. The other was Finn's rabies vaccination.

Diego's stomach had plummeted when he'd found the requirements for transporting pets across the Canadian border. Dogs were permitted, but not without documentation of their rabies shots. He couldn't ask Finn to endure the needle and there was no way to know what horrible reaction his body might have to the vaccine. In a bit of underhandedness that still had him losing sleep, Diego had picked up a stray to use as a proxy. The dog got his vaccination, Diego got the papers he needed for Finn, and Tia Carmen took the stray to one of the no-kill shelters.

For all her brave words about getting Finn out of the city, she had cried over him the night before, soothing her own anxieties by stuffing him full of food. She had pulled Finn's head down to hers when they said good night at her door and whispered in his ear. Diego could have sworn he caught the words, "Take good care of him."

Now Diego hesitated at his own door, mentally checking things off. Luggage. Water. Laptop. Keys. Documents. Coffee pot was off. Dishes washed. Why did he have this knot the size of a basketball in his stomach? He shivered, tried to shake the feeling of something lurking over his shoulder, and locked the door.

* * * *

"Diego, I don't feel well at all."

Not even ten miles outside the city. Damn.

"You want to lie down in the back?"

"I want to get out of this accursed box and be sick somewhere."

The tires shrieked as Diego wrestled the

truck to a stop on the shoulder. He raced around to Finn's side and lifted him down, narrowly sidestepping what Finn could no longer hold in his stomach.

"My apologies," Finn murmured when he finished.

"You sure you can do this?"

"Yes. I must. Perhaps if we had something to muffle the iron's effects?"

"Such as?"

"A silver shield would be best."

"I'm afraid I left all the arms and armor at home. What else?"

"Dragon skin? Were-pelt? Silk?"

"That last one we can manage." Diego slid back the truck bed's cover and retrieved his silk bathrobe from the suitcase. He'd only packed the thing because it took up less room than terrycloth. The scarlet and gold threads sparked in the streetlight when he spread the cloth on the back seat. What an odd fate for

Mitch's last Christmas present.

Finn settled with a huff and curled up with his tail over his nose. Only one paw protruded when Diego finished covering him with the rest of the robe.

"Better?"

"Yes, much. Are we close yet?"

Diego resisted the urge to roll his eyes. "I warned you we'd have to drive all day."

"I had hoped you were exaggerating."

Five hours later, at a rest area outside Portland, Diego pulled over again. Finn had started to wheeze.

"We're about halfway there." Diego clipped the leash on for propriety's sake and carried Finn into the shade of the picnic area.

"Then why… have we… stopped?"

"Sh, don't talk here. Someone might hear you."

"Aren't you… the storyteller?" Finn gasped. "You'd concoct… some explanation."

Diego sat down in confusion next to his 'dog'. "I'm not usually a liar, you know."

"All storytellers… are liars. Part… of the craft."

"But…" Diego considered while he stroked the thick ruff of fur around Finn's neck. "Fiction isn't lying. Everyone knows it's imaginary. It's not as if the writer's being dishonest and misleading the reader."

"Though it's still not true."

"Well… no, it's not."

"Honest lying." Finn laid his head on Diego's thigh. "I like that."

"It's not… oh, never mind."

A shadow fell across Diego's legs. He glanced up, startled, to see a little girl, her hair a mass of unruly brown curls, staring intently at Finn. "My dad says your dog's a wolf."

"Melissa! That's not what I said." A burly man strode up behind her, a blush visible under his tan. "I'm sorry. Kids. You know." He crouched down next to Finn. "What I said was he looks like a wolf-hybrid. Is he? I've had a couple come through the office. None as beautiful as this one."

Diego let out a soft breath. "He didn't exactly come with papers."

"Ah. Stray? Rescued?"

"I spotted him in a bad spot and took him home."

The man grinned. "Sorry. Don't mean to pry. I'm a vet, can't help asking sometimes." He ruffled Finn's ears. The feathered tail thumped the ground shamelessly. "He looks a little under the weather."

"He's, um, carsick," Diego offered, certain that wouldn't wash with a veterinarian.

The vet nodded. "Happens to lots of big dogs. Wait there a second for me, all right?" He went to his truck and returned with a bottle half the size of Diego's palm. "Ginger root. No more than three drops to settle his stomach."

"Thank you. Look, I can't just take this from you—"

"Nah, forget it. Letting me take a look at your dog's enough. I've never seen anything like him."

Finn lifted his head to let out a short bark.

"He said thank you, too, Daddy," the little girl said with a laugh.

"Probably so. You have far to go today?"

"About six more hours," Diego answered. "Just outside Fundy National Park."

"He may need another dose before then. You two be careful up there. Don't let him get away from you; he'll want to join his wild cousins."

"I'll keep it in mind."

Finn took the ginger without protest and settled back in his silk cocoon, his breathing quieter.

Mid-afternoon Thursday, only two cars

idled ahead of Diego at the Canadian border crossing. A short wait, but the patrol officers would be able to take their time. Diego reminded himself that he had nothing to worry about. He was transporting a dog, not drugs. What was the worst they could say? 'You sure that's a dog, sir? Looks like an illegal immigrant pooka to me' seemed unlikely.

He handed over his passport and Finn's vaccine certification and tried to still his thudding heart.

The border officer glanced at his papers, looked him over, disappeared into the booth a moment and then returned without handing the documents back.

"Mind if I take a look in the truck bed, sir?"

"Not at all. Go right ahead."

The officer slid the cover back, poked around for a few moments and closed it again. He sauntered back to Diego's rolled-down window, tapping the passport against his palm. "What's in the back seat, sir?"

Diego turned to look without thinking. "Oh. That's my dog."

"Your dog."

"Yes. He doesn't like the car, so he hides under there. Finn, could you stick your head out so the nice man can see you?"

Finn nosed the silk far enough aside to expose his head but instead of waving them on, the officer's mouth drew down farther. "Pull over to the side, please, sir."

"Is there a problem, officer?"

"Just pull over there, sir. We'll be right with you."

Oh, God, please, please let this be a random search. He parked the truck, turned off the ignition and sat paralyzed, both hands clutching the steering wheel.

"Diego?" A wet nose nuzzled his ear. "You're going to throw yourself into a fit. Deep breath. Another. That's my braveheart. If we're in a bad spot, you must tell me what needs to be done."

"Don't do anything, Finn, please. You're a dog. Act like a dog."

Finn growled.

"A nice dog."

Diego turned and let out a nervous laugh. Finn sat on the back seat, tongue lolling out, tail wagging, with the bathrobe still around his shoulders.

"Perfect."

The border guard brought reinforcements; four uniformed men surrounded the truck.

"Step out of the car, sir. Hands on top of your head."

Diego eased out as instructed, hoping his knees would hold him. "Officer, if there's something I've done…"

"Anything on you I should know about,

sir?" The officer ignored the question as he patted Diego down. "Weapons? Needles?"

"No. Look, I've…"

The officer pulled his pills and the bottle of ginger root out of Diego's jacket pocket. "What're these?"

"The prescription's seizure medication. The other bottle the vet gave me for my dog."

"Run that, Mark." The first officer tossed both containers to a second, who disappeared inside the customs building.

"I… excuse me. Please. I need those." I did take one this morning. Didn't I?

"All right, Mr Sandoval. If that's really your dog, call him out here." The officer opened the back door.

Diego tried to whistle but his mouth was too dry. "Finn, come out here, boy. Out here by me."

A scrabble of claws and a whimper told him Finn was trying, but the truck frame must have given him pause. After two more tries, he jumped out and landed in a heap on the concrete.

"Please, he's sick. This is cruel."

"Call him over."

"Finn, come here to me." Diego crouched and had no sooner held out his arms than they were full of wriggling, black-furred canine. Finn licked his face with pleased little whines, his tail flailing back and forth like a windshield wiper on speed.

"Oh, come on, Greg," one of the other officers said. "It's a dog, not a wolf. Look at the eyes. And if it's not his, I'll eat my shorts. Hell, I'll eat your shorts."

Diego's legs gave way. He sat down hard and buried his face in the thick ruff of neck fur. Officer Greg put a hand on his shoulder and Finn snarled.

"Okay, sorry. Easy there, eh?" He backed up with a laugh. "Sorry, Mr Sandoval.

We had to be sure. We've had reports of illegal exotics going back and forth across the border. You know, animals people keep as pets that they're crazy to. Panthers. Tigers. Wolves. Your dog, well, I thought he was a wolf."

"The vet said he might have some wolf in him," Diego managed, still clutching Finn tight. "But he was a stray, so I don't really know."

"These are as advertised on the label." Officer Mark had returned and handed back the medications. "Looks to me like he's got Belgian in him. That deep chest."

"Maybe some Newfoundland with that coat," added one of the others. "He's a beauty, Mr Sandoval. No doubt."

"So we're okay to go, then?"

"Oh, yeah, sure. Sorry about the mix up there."

"It's all right, officers. Could someone help me get him back in?"

With a few more rounds of apologies for Diego and effusive praise for Finn, they lifted Finn back onto his silk and covered him up.

"That really helps his car sickness?"

Diego nodded. "Seems to. He hasn't thrown up since New York."

When the border lay a mile behind them, Finn finally spoke again. "That's twice today, my hero."

"Twice for what?"

"That you have successfully misled without telling a single falsehood. You do indeed have the gift."

"I don't think misleading people is something to be proud of."

Silence fell for another half mile. Then, "Is it a human thing? Is it simply right and natural for you to be ashamed of what you are?"

"I think you're confusing morality and shame."

"I think you're a great fool to try to

separate them," Finn muttered. He shifted with a heavy sigh. "Diego, my head throbs. My joints ache. My eyes burn. Please forgive my churlishness. Tell me again about the wild place."

Diego had read the guidebook entry aloud to him enough times to have memorized it. "Fundy National Park is over two hundred square kilometers of mixed conifer and hardwood forest rising sharply from the misty coastline to the Caledonia highlands..."

* * * *

Finn had drifted off during the recitation of the park's virtues, so Diego spent the last five hours of the drive in quiet solitude. The ever-thickening stands of evergreens edged closer on either side of the road with every passing mile. Majestic and beautiful, certainly, but the sheer volume of trees unsettled Diego. Their branches intertwined as if they locked arms against intruders, dark, ancient sentinels guarding their secrets with jealous zeal.

The yellow caution signs about moose crossings didn't help one bit.

Asleep in his silken cocoon, Finn missed the changes in the landscape, but Diego didn't have the heart to wake him. The robe rose and fell with his shallow, rapid breaths, interrupted by the occasional twitch and whimper.

"Almost there, almost," Diego whispered, when Finn cried out in his sleep. "Hang on for me."

The sun rested on the tips of the conifers by the time he reached the pastor's house, three miles south of the cabin. Armed with the keys, meticulous directions including caveats about the largest craters in the road, and a casserole for dinner, Diego returned to the truck to remove Finn's collar. His ears twitched but he didn't even lift his head.

"You could shift back now if you wanted."

"Perhaps later," Finn whispered. "I'm so tired."

The last few miles Diego took at a crawl. The main road abandoned, the approach to the cabin lay on an uneven, gravel track. Every hard jolt wrenched a moan from the backseat. The trees stood thick here, evergreens interspersed with birch and maple. He had expected quiet, an eerie silence, but sounds saturated the air. Cars, buses and jackhammers had been replaced by chirps, peeps, and whistles.

"Noisy neighborhood," Diego muttered, his unease growing with every sound he couldn't identify.

After a final turn, the cabin loomed before them. 'Cabin' was an incredible misnomer. At least this monstrosity had been built out of wood, but there the resemblance to a one-room log structure ended. The array of windows on the second floor announced the existence of several bedrooms. A three-car garage nestled smugly on the left side. A flagstone-lined barbecue patio and a massive veranda graced the front of the house.

I might need a ball of twine to find my way back out of there.

Diego carried Finn from his metal prison to lay him on the grass while he unpacked the truck. Only Finn's furred chest moved with the slow rise and fall of his breathing.

"You want me to carry you in?" Diego crouched beside him when all the luggage and bags were safely inside. "Or maybe bring you dinner out here?"

Finn's eyes remained shut. "Leave me here. I'm not hungry. Go rest."

"It'll get cold out here."

"Diego, I never lived inside a building before I guested with you. Do you think Irish winters are warm?"

"No, but…"

"I said leave me be. Gods. Deaf as well as stubborn."

"Fine, fine." Diego chewed on his bottom lip as he walked back to the house. Finn's voice stopped him when he reached the steps.

"Diego?"

"Yes?"

"It is a beautiful place."

"Everything you wanted?"

"More than I ever dared hope for."

Chapter 8: Taking the City Out of the Boy

Finn shifted back to his own form, a painful, tedious process after his daylong confinement, but a relief all the same. He rolled spread eagle onto his back to get as much of his skin in contact with the earth as possible, opening himself to the flows. Fingers digging into the dirt, he reached into the depths for the strongest veins of magic. Relief flooded through every scrap of him.

The cacophony of scents brought tears to his eyes—damp grass, new leaves, wildflowers sweet and woody, the sharp tang of insects, hints of territorial musk, humus, and loam. He turned his gaze upward and nearly sobbed aloud.

Great Dagda. Stars.

He hadn't seen stars since he'd woken. With all the horrors confronting him, he'd been afraid to ask Diego if the stars still shone. As if an evil fog dissipated, his senses sprang back to heart-pounding clarity.

A bat fluttered against the house in her hunt for mosquitoes. Three deer picked their cautious way through a nearby clearing. Hundreds of crickets sang. An owl called across the treetops—

"Finn!"

The houselights flared, blocking out the stars. Diego barreled down the front steps in nothing but the delightfully short pants he wore to bed. Lovely sight if Diego hadn't been white with shock.

"I'm here, my hero," Finn called. "What's amiss?"

"I… there was…" Diego shook his head as he did when he became flustered. "I heard a scream. I thought it was you."

"A scream?"

The owl called again and Diego stabbed

a finger toward the woods. "There!"

"Ah, that would be the baine sidhe come to rip your soul away."

"Banshees are real, too?"

Diego's expression held such a mix of horror and disbelief Finn found himself unable to continue his small mischief. "They did, but there are none here. That is merely an owl calling for her mate."

"That horrible shriek is an owl? I thought they just hooted."

Finn reached over to pat his foot. "Listen a moment." A mile distant, another owl called in answer. "That's her male answering."

"*Dios.*" Diego plunked down on the grass shivering. "I never realized the woods would be so loud."

"The man sleeps like the dead through machines thundering past his window all night and thinks a few crickets too loud?" Finn muttered.

A rabbit rustled in the leaves and Diego startled, edging closer. *Take good care of him,* the wisewoman had said. *He needs a friend so badly now.* He watched the lean muscles in Diego's arms stand out in hard relief as he shivered. Such an endearing contradiction of vulnerable strength, but it was the white-hot spark of Diego, such a brief flame but oh-so-bright that drew Finn like a hapless moth to the bonfire.

"You should go back in. You'll catch your death out here."

"Just for a bit. Maybe I'll get a blanket and sit out here with you awhile. Keep you company."

I'm not the one needing company, m'boy. Finn rose onto his elbows. "Help me up, then. I'll come in with you. Perhaps it is a mite chilly out here tonight."

"No, no, you need to stay outside, don't you? To get better?"

"It is enough to be out of that blasted city." He stretched the truth, but not too much. "Come. You're turning blue."

Inside, Finn found he approved of the open main room. Almost like being outside, windows comprised one wall and much of the high ceiling. An ottoman large enough for four men to curl up together stood in front of the fireplace and Finn indicated he would sleep there.

"Bring your blankets. Sleep with me."

Diego frowned, hesitating. "Finn, I don't think…"

"Just sleep. I give you my solemn promise. You are distressed and will rest better with someone by your side, I think."

"I don't suppose you'd consider putting on some clothes?"

"More than willing if it puts you at ease."

After some thuds and rustlings upstairs,

Diego returned with a pile of blankets and the soft, black pants he had given Finn to sleep in that first night. *Small victories. Take what you can get.*

"How did you know the owl was a she? And who she was calling to?" Diego asked, as he slid under the blankets beside him.

"I speak owl quite fluently. And deer and boar and duck and mosquito, to name a few."

"Wait. How could anyone learn to speak mosquito?"

"Easy enough when you've been one. Though I don't recommend it." He wanted so badly to pull Diego close and hold him chest to chest, but he had promised. Most promises he wouldn't care whether he kept them or not, but a promise to Diego was somehow different.

"I thought it was too difficult to become something that small."

"When I'm ill, yes. When I'm whole and

sound, it's possible. I tried mosquito form one summer simply to see what it would be like. The end result was rather messy and nasty."

"What happened?"

"A thrush ate me. I had to choose between escape and being digested, which leaves no guarantees of being able to piece one's self back together afterward. So I escaped."

Diego gazed at him with rapt attention. *Gods, it's hard not to kiss him.* "How?"

"I became a crow. Bit too large for the thrush to hold in his stomach. As I said, the results were messy. Lost my taste for bird for quite some time after that."

Diego's nose wrinkled and then he laughed. "No, really. You're making that up."

"Would that I were, boyo. But it's a good story either way."

"It is." A smile appeared, though Diego's gaze had gone far into the distance.

"You've had a thought."

"I've had the start of an idea. Let me keep it for a little."

Moonlight slid along the floor as Finn identified one night noise after another for his city-dwelling friend and soon Diego fell asleep. Finn rested beside him, almost content, and took his hand in a gentle grip. He didn't think Diego would consider that breaking his promise.

* * * *

Diego woke to the sun bathing his face and the vague recollection that someone should have been with him.

"Mitch?"

After the inevitable disorientation of waking on an ottoman subsided, he wrapped a blanket around his shoulders and got up to look for Finn. The pooka sprawled on a chair on the veranda, feet propped up on the railing, lazing in the sunlight like a contented cat, thick fall of blue back hair cascading over the chair back to the wood planks.

He opened one eye when Diego sat beside him. "I sleep beside you all night, and still you call for him when you wake?"

Diego felt the flush in his cheeks. "Sorry. You heard me all the way out here?"

"My hearing has returned to its proper state now. Yes, I heard. I can hear a fly walking on the roof at the back of the house." Finn sat up and turned to him. "I wanted to brew you a pot of that vile stuff you drink in the morning but I couldn't identify which machine to use."

"Thank you for the thought, but maybe you better leave the new machines to me. What would you like for breakfast?"

"I've, ah, already eaten." Finn avoided his eyes.

"Oh. Should I ask?"

"I truly don't think you want the details. But perhaps it will be a few chirps quieter this evening for you."

"You're right. I don't want to hear any more. You couldn't wait for me to make you pancakes or something?"

"I was famished. And you slept so peacefully. Besides which, crickets are quite nourishing. A bit larger than I'm used to. Somewhat nuttier…"

"Stop right there. Please."

Finn followed him into the kitchen. "Would do you some good, too. All those city poisons have smothered you."

"Um, maybe so, but I'd never keep them down." Diego puzzled over the coffeemaker's array of mysterious buttons.

"This is a much larger eating room than yours. Is it meant for a large family? Do they have feasts in here? What's that odd thing with its feet in the bowl?"

"You're chatty this morning," Diego said as he located the cabinet with coffee and filters.

"Something on your mind?"

Finn pulled a chair out from the table and flung himself into it. "Are you or are you not going to tell me what you thought of last night?"

"That's been itching at you all this time?"

"Yes." Finn drummed his fingers on the table, a red tinge in his eyes. "So will you tell me or do I resort to extreme measures?"

"I'm not fond of being threatened…"

"Please tell me!" Finn dropped to his knees, arms spread in supplication. "The look in your eyes intrigued me so. Please, before my head bursts from wondering."

Diego let out a laugh, startled by the degree of Finn's desperation. Hard to resist a handsome man on his knees. He had to turn away to hide his growing erection against the counter.

"Hold out for me a couple minutes. Wait

right there." He went upstairs, threw on some clothes and returned with his digital camera and his palm-sized tape recorder.

Finn sighed. "More machines. What do these do?"

"This one takes pictures."

"Where does it take them?"

"No, I mean it creates pictures."

"That little thing? Does it have tiny hands to draw?"

"Stand still and I'll show you."

Finn stopped his agitated pacing and stood with his feet planted, arms crossed over his chest.

He already looks better. I swear he's filled out some...

Diego took the shot and then turned the screen to Finn. "You see? Like in the magazines you like so much. I don't know exactly how it works but it's like taking an impression of a moment in time."

"A footprint of light," Finn concluded, tilting his head this way and that to see the picture. "Was I truly scowling so?"

"I'm afraid you were."

"This is all quite fascinating, but there's more to it, if I'm not mistaken."

"Yes. I love hearing your stories. I'd like to compile some. Put a book together of your life for everyone to read, illustrated with your likeness. Probably not with actual photos. They'd want an illustrator, I'd think, but with you as the model."

Finn's forehead wrinkled. "You think that's wise?"

"I won't do anything without your consent. But if you're worried about exposure, I don't think there'll be a problem. Fiction is honest lying, you said. And I got all bent out of shape, but you're right. People want to suspend their disbelief while they read but with the understanding that it's not true. If I present it as fiction, no one would ever dream it's true."

"You're deviousness astounds me," Finn said in feigned shock, and then he grinned. "I like that in a companion. But truly, why would you want to do this?"

"To save my writing career. That sounds really mercenary, doesn't it?" Diego sank into the nearest chair, the realization of what he asked hitting hard. "I'm sorry. It's a horrible thing to use you like that. I can't believe I even thought about it."

Finn perched hipshot on the table and put a hand under Diego's chin to lift his head. "It's a wickedly marvelous idea. And if I can be your inspiration, I am more than pleased. Diego, look at me. Your channels are all snarled. Perhaps if you do this, the flotsam and debris will be swept away and let the streams flow again."

"Thank you. I have been in a nasty slump lately. But you have to understand. This came to me as something that would be a commercial success. Money, you understand? The something different that Miriam keeps prodding me to do."

"Just so. Even better. If I can help put food on your table, I will tell you a thousand stories."

Diego explained the tape recorder and once Finn had heard his own voice, there was no talking him out of it. Tape recorder, camera, Diego, and all had to be dragged out for long walks in the woods so Finn could think better. Pictures of Finn were better outdoors as well, the dappled sunlight giving him a fallen angel mystique.

* * * *

By the end of the week, Finn's ribs had disappeared under a sleek layer of lean muscle, his body returning to the sculpted perfection

Diego had caught hints of in the city. He had to admit, the change of scenery proved beneficial for them both. Despite nasty surprises like running face first into cobwebs and often getting his socks wet, he ate more, slept better, and began to come home from their walks refreshed rather than exhausted.

* * * *

Normally, Diego would have agonized over how to begin but with Finn's deep voice as his constant companion while he typed, the book seemed to compile itself.

> *Preface:*
> *I first met the pooka on the Brooklyn Bridge. Though desperately ill from pollution and iron poisoning, and half crazed with starvation, he still managed*

to find the courtesy to introduce himself and the humor to grant me a smile. His courage won me over and my trust has won his.

With the pooka's full consent, this book contains selected transcripts of taped conversations with him in which I've asked questions about his life and his adventures. As far as I can ascertain, this is the first serious foray any human has made into pooka research. Since they are, by nature, solitary and suspicious of strangers, this is not altogether shocking. However, our pooka, whom I will refer to as Thistle to protect his privacy, would like to set the record straight.

This then, is his life, in

his own words.

Chapter 1

Beginnings

Why don't we go back to the start. Do you know anything about your birth? Your parents?

"Pookas have no parents. Unless you count the Earth herself as our mother, for surely we must have sprung from somewhere. We simply are. One day I was not. The next day, I was."

Do you have childhoods? Or are you fully grown when you spring forth, or parthenogenesize, or however you come into being?

"Oh, I think I take your meaning. I don't recall ever

being a smaller version of myself. And I have never met a pooka cub. Difficult to say. Perhaps I still am a child and will grow into something else."

Diego inserted a picture here of Finn sitting shirtless at the kitchen table, his long hair pulled over one shoulder. He captioned it: *Thistle empties the saltshaker out on the table and draws in the salt with his fingers while he talks.*

So you've never had children?

(A long silence on the tape while Thistle leaves the room and returns somewhat flushed and agitated.)

"I'm not certain."

But you may have?

"Perhaps. It's a time-honored tradition for country girls to blame the local pooka when they are with child and wish to protect a human lover. If every girl who claimed me as their child's father spoke truly, I would have an ocean full of half-blood progeny. But most of them I never lay with. Or did so when they were out of season. There was once, though..."

Yes?

"I have a particular weakness. Ach, you'll laugh. It's catnip."

(I'm ashamed to say I do laugh.)

"Fine, fine. All too amusing. But it has the same effect on me that a cask of wine

would on you. I came across this great, green patch of it one day and fully intended just a sniff. Mayhap, a bit of a roll. But it was late Spring and the sun was warm and once I had my nose in the stuff, I lost all track of my feet.

"So there I lay, head floating, feeling pleasantly numb, when a small herd of beautiful young maidens happens by. At least I believe they were beautiful. It may have been a catnip view of things."

While you were lying there stark naked?

"Well, now, what do you think, boyo? It's not as if I usually carry clothes with me for such occasions. Yes, in my

natural state, stretched out helpless on the ground. They took a liking to me, cooed and fussed over me, but when they realized I was intoxicated rather than ill, they started to..."

(I've edited out much of what follows to avoid censorship issues.)

"... so a few months later when I spot them at the river again and all five of them are carrying, what am I to think?"

Did you ever see any of the children? Did they look like yours?

"One girl-child, perhaps. Raven-haired, a fey, wild thing. She lived well over a century."

But you never told her?

"No. Should I have? I

don't know what good it would have done her." (Thistle lays his head on his arms—another long pause on the tape.) "Is there ice cream? I think I'd like some about now."

"Diego? Are we going out today? The rain has all but ceased."

He looked up to find Finn leaning in the doorway in his favorite black jeans. They were the only concession he was willing to make clothing-wise, in case they ran into other hikers.

"Give me a minute to finish up. And let me find my boots."

Finn held up the hiking boots in his left hand and the camera in his right.

"All right, I'm coming!" Diego surrendered with a laugh.

Mist curtained the woods that afternoon, creating phantom shapes in the distance and making Diego uncertain of the way, especially since Finn kept dashing off ahead. He returned every time, excited by each new find—a rabbit's warren, a tree frog, a handful of blackberries—but Diego couldn't shake the feeling that each time he raced off into the swirling silver-gray, he would never come back.

Would that be a bad thing? This is where he belongs, not with me.

He trudged on another few steps, listening for the light rustle of Finn's feet skimming over the leaves. *But I'd miss him, dammit.*

A sudden tightening in his chest overwhelmed him, and he sat down hard on a fallen tree trunk. A hand cupped his cheek. Finn had come back without a sound.

"You're ill today? Diego, you should have said so."

"I'm fine. I am." He grabbed Finn's hand and pulled him down on the log. "Just sit still a second, could you? I can't keep up."

"You don't need to, my hero. I will always know where you are." Finn hooked an arm around his shoulders and hugged him tight, shivers running through his long frame.

"What is it? Did something scare you?"

"No… not precisely. I thought I heard something in the far distance. But I couldn't make it out, and then your pain stabbed at me."

"I'm sorry. Oh, God, Finn, I never realized you could…"

"Hush." Finn put a finger over his lips. "I block it out most times. It was simply that I listened so intently."

"Do you know what it was?" He gazed into those black eyes, thousands of fathoms deep, and became acutely aware of Finn's thigh pressed against his.

"No, it's gone. I think I imagined it." Finn's hand slipped to the side of his face, index finger caressing the curves of his ear. "You're so warm." He brushed his lips over Diego's, feather-light.

"Finn…"

"Yes, yes. My apologies." Finn held up his hands and backed off. "Carried away in the moment. Are we going to the river or do I take you back to the house?"

"Let's go on. I want a picture of you by the rocks. Or maybe on them. We'll have to see if anything comes out in this light."

Finn smiled and pulled him to his feet. "And if not, I still get my swim."

Chapter 9: Hope and Despair

Diego set his coffee on the counter and sneezed again. "I hope you don't mind, but I'm staying in today."

"Ah. I forget that the damp isn't the best thing for you." Finn leaned against the counter drinking milk. He'd bought Finn his own bottle, still sold in glass containers in the local stores, so he could stop nagging about the proper use of drinking vessels. "You stay warm and dry. I'll go out on my own."

"You think that's a good idea? What if something happens? Or the park rangers think you're a vagrant? You don't have any identification and no way to contact me."

Finn pondered this a moment, put the bottle down and stalked off.

What now? Did I offend him?

He returned with his bright, Cheshire smile and his collar. "I'll go out in my canine skin today. That way, on the fingernail-thin chance that something might happen, I have your name and number around my neck and the park rangers can call you, yes?"

"Yes. You're too damn clever." Diego took the collar with a chuckle and turned to pour himself more coffee. When he turned back, Dog Finn sat on the kitchen floor, tail thumping on the granite tiles. "Oh. I guess you want to go right now."

Finn leaped to all fours and let out a happy bark, jumping around Diego's feet in manic canine joy.

"Whoa! Settle down and let me put this on." Diego dropped to one knee and fastened the collar. A sudden surge of emotion welled up. He swallowed hard, threw his arms around Finn's neck and hugged him tight. "You be careful. Don't stay out too long."

He got a long, wet tongue in his ear for his troubles.

"You worry too much. Go write. All will be well."

The conifers stood draped in mourning veils of fog. Diego shivered as he watched Finn lope off into the woods, one hand raised to wave when Finn turned back to bark farewell.

Why had he pushed Finn away again the day before? His reasons for resistance had edged over to plain stubborn. That moment in the woods, he should have grabbed him and kissed him stupid. Instead, he left them both frustrated and lonely. Finn hid his hurt well, but he never quite covered the little wince every time he was refused.

To hell with Mitch. To hell with putting up barricades because of the pain. And to hell with all of the manufactured reasonable explanations. Finn couldn't have made it any clearer. He wanted Diego, despite his neuroses and his infirmity. Someone warm, caring, passionate, intelligent and understanding offered himself freely. What did it matter that he wasn't human? What did it matter that this might be a brief, heated affair? They needed each other now, in so many ways, and he was selfish to keep shoving Finn away.

Enough was enough. Tonight he'd make dinner, with candlelight, flowers, the works. Then when they were content and relaxed, maybe lazing by the fire, he would let whatever happened happen.

Decision made, he threw himself into his work with a vengeance.

Chapter 3 Diet and Habitat

You seem to be omnivorous.

"Pardon?"

Omnivorous. You'll eat just about anything.

"I couldn't eat that blasted pretzel you tried to feed me. And those long things that were supposedly meat? Heated dogs? Disgusting."

What I mean is, you eat meat and plant matter and fish and insects. Like a bear. An opportunistic feeder.

"Oh, yes. All of those things. Of course, it depends on the form I'm wearing, too. I can't very well eat meat when I'm in horse form. Doesn't work well with that kind of stomach. While the wildcat shape doesn't much appreciate thistles and hay. One has to take advantage of the season and the food available."

Do you ever take food from humans?

"I have fed from around human habitations, if that's what you mean. There do tend to be numerous temptations thereabouts. Lovely fields of wheat. Fat chickens sitting in pens waiting for someone hungry to happen by. Apple trees and cabbages and these marvelous tubs with a stick on top where you can get butter if you time things right. But humans, present company excepted, aren't good at sharing. They come after you with sharp bits of iron and sticks if they see you eating around their homes. Best to avoid such unpleasant scenes."

But isn't there a tradition about leaving out a bowl of cream for the local pooka?

"Ah, such a hospitable tradition that was. I do so love cream. Only elderly grandmothers still observed it in the time before I slept, though. And then the household cats usually lapped it up before I could get to it."

Diego inserted the photo of Finn stretched out naked on a flat rock by the river. One knee bent up to obscure Finn's genitals, he hoped the picture would be viewed as artistic rather than pornographic. The mist-shrouded river, the water rushing around the edges of the rock outcropping, the dark woods in the background he thought perfect for hinting at the hidden depths of the photo's subject.

Late that morning, he sent Miriam a short blurb about the book concept, the first three chapters, and all of the photos. The phone rang before an hour passed.

"Diego? Oh, my God, is that Finn in these pictures?"

He held the phone away to preserve his hearing. "Um, yes."

Colorful swearing followed for a full thirty seconds. "Well, shit, kiddo. No wonder you changed your mind and decided to keep him all to yourself. Greedy bastard. He's gorgeous."

"Maybe I'll introduce you someday."

"You better if you know what's good for you. What'd you do, raid the Playgirl model stable?"

"Not quite. Did you even look at the book idea or just the pictures?"

Miriam's volume decreased. "It's a keeper, hon. I smell pay dirt. I can pitch with what you sent but what are you looking at for completion time?"

"Two weeks. Maybe three. I've got most of the material. Just compiling right now."

"Attaboy. This could be my easiest sale in years. These fantasy 'natural histories', they're hot right now. Dragons. Faeries. Should be able to get it out in time for the whole Christmas, hard-cover, gift-book season." Miriam paused. "Is he willing to sign a release for those photos?"

Diego's heart stuttered. A release. From someone who shouldn't exist. "I'd like to use the photos as a suggestion. Maybe get an illustrator for the book? Finn's a bit shy. I don't think he wants the actual pictures used."

"Yeah, right, shy. I can see that."

He laughed. "Not with me."

"'K, sweetie. Stand back and watch me work. I'll have something for you soon."

Miriam's confidence soothed his fears. This would work. He'd never harbored any illusions about being rich and famous as some starry-eyed authors did, but a livable income would be a relief.

Finn might be home soon. 'Home' together with 'Finn' sounded so permanent and comfortable. If he had some money, he could buy a little house somewhere away from any urban sprawl. Minnesota, maybe. Or Montana.

"One step at a time. No building air castles again." But the possibility of lying in Finn's arms that night sent a rush of desire right down to his knees. He clutched the desk, dizzy from the sudden redistribution of blood.

With a soft laugh, he tugged on the leg of his jeans and threw himself back into his work.

* * * *

The problem with taking on dog form was the lack of focus. Dog senses yanked the mind this way and that with disorienting results. The sheer joy of overloaded senses, though, alleviated any annoyance.

Finn's canine lope devoured ground while he struggled in the throes of tumultuous ecstasy to keep his thoughts in order. Sights, scents, and sounds assaulted him like waves in a storm.

Moss
lichen
owl fewmet
(mouse)
bunchberry
wasp wasp wasp
green snake
(mouse)
spruce
squirrel
distant human
MOOSE
flash of falcon overhead!
(mouse)
raccoon spore
fir

primrose

roar of river River RIVER...

Rush and sparkle, crash and dance, the Pointe Wolf River leapt into view. He froze on the bank, legs trembling. The river song, sweet and clear, skittered over his skin, pulled at his bones. Oh gods, oh gods, so glorious it rips the heart.

He closed his eyes, pulled himself inward, and slid into the river as an otter.

* * * *

The groceries shifted with ominous thuds when the truck hit another crater. Diego winced and sent up a prayer that the cream had landed on top. The trip into what passed for a town nearby had taken longer than he'd intended. Items he took for granted back home, like arugula, prompted raised brows and puzzled looks here. A few compromises and substitutions later, he returned to the house, relieved to find he'd beaten Finn back.

Not that it mattered, but he did want dinner to be a surprise. If Finn were there, his ravenous curiosity would drive him underfoot during the entire dinner preparation.

A rich strawberry cheesecake, a salad with currants and walnuts and a batch of cornbread later, (the steaks would have to wait until Finn arrived) Diego turned to the dining area. He considered setting up at one end of the ten-person table but discarded the thought. The occasion called for a more intimate space. He found a card table in a closet and a deep burgundy tablecloth the right size, black china place settings, and delicate wine glasses with gold bubbles set in the stems. Two islands of milky white completed the setting—one the vase holding the wildflowers and the other the bowl that would hold Finn's cream.

Diego hummed as he climbed the stairs

to get ready, anticipation dancing through him.

* * * *

The otter shot downriver. His whiskers tingled with the vibration around him, alerting him to fish and crustaceans, upcoming rocks and rapids. Without slowing, he snatched a fish from its hiding place under an outcropping and rose to the surface.

He climbed onto a rock, fish head clutched in his sharp teeth. Cool, glorious fish. Smooth, soft meat and the crunch of small bones. Sun-warmed granite. Splash of clear water. Scent of algae. The flows of life sluiced through him; the patterns of interconnected magic leaped out clear and bright for him again. The small magics of grass and fern. The larger flow that comprised the river. The...

The feeling reached him as it had the day before, a keening hunger in the distance. Not an audible sensation but a humming inside his head. Something… something…

Gods.

He leaped onto the bank as a deer and raced into the woods. Another magical being trapped like himself on this side of the Veil. Somewhere in these woods. The threads from this other mind emanated strange vibrations, nothing he had met before, but he had to find whoever it was.

I am not alone.

* * * *

Diego fidgeted and glanced at the clock again. Six-fifteen. Five minutes later than the last time he checked. Finn would stay out longer without someone tagging along to worry about, of course. Still, his impatience grew as the sun came to rest atop the conifer tips and then penetrated them.

He turned on the television, channel surfed, turned it off. He opened the front door to check outside, then came back in to fuss with the table for the hundredth time.

After eight, a gripping anxiety lodged in his stomach. What if something had happened? What if some hunter had mistaken Finn for a wolf and shot him? Was it hunting season up here? Were they allowed to shoot wolves?

Flashlight in hand, he trudged out into the woods to check the familiar trails. He didn't dare go too far. No moon shone and the woods were an inky black so thick it crawled on his skin.

"Finn!"

He called until his throat was raw but no one called back in greeting or distress. Only the owl shrieked at him from her tree, but whether she tried to tell him something or warn him off, he couldn't decipher. He didn't speak owl.

Over an hour later, he trudged back to

the house. Finn must have stayed out to enjoy the night air. He loved nighttime here. Probably counting the stars.

Diego told himself these things, stubbornly avoiding the one thought he could not face. Finn would be back. Soon. In the morning.

Do I lock the door? But what if he comes back and can't get in? Will he think I've locked him out on purpose? Though if I leave the door open, who knows what's out there.

Axe murderers came to mind. He compromised and locked the door but stayed downstairs to sleep on the oversized ottoman in case Finn knocked.

The ottoman held traces of Finn's scent. He supposed it was as close to sleeping with Finn as he would get that evening. The whole thing was his fault, though, so he tried to shove his disappointment into a dark corner. He should have told Finn he was making dinner, should have sent him off with a kiss and a promise if he expected him back by dinnertime.

He woke with the sun to the uncomfortable sensation of having slept in his clothes. *Oh, no. I must not have heard him when he came back.*

"Finn?" He flung open the front door, expecting, hoping to find Finn on the grass. Nothing. No long, lean body stretched out near the house, no muddy footprints on the veranda, no sign he had been home at all. "Finn!"

Only the crickets and birds answered.

Diego slumped in one of the porch chairs and scrubbed his hands over his face. "Where are you, dammit?"

He retraced their usual trails again in daylight. If Finn lay hurt somewhere, he would have missed him in the dark. Again he called and called with no response. He had just come back out of the trees when his cell vibrated in his jacket pocket.

"Hello?"

"Mr Sandoval?"

"Yes?"

"This is Tara McHenry with the Park Service at Fundy. Are you somewhere near the park?"

"Yes," he answered when he could breathe again. "Yes, I'm staying at Miriam Thorpe's house on the northwest side. Is everything all right? Did you find my dog?"

The moment's hesitation made his stomach sink to his feet.

"We… we found his collar, Mr Sandoval. On the bank of the Pointe Wolf. By some class five rapids. I'm sorry, sir, it doesn't look good."

"No sign of him?" he whispered.

"What does your dog look like? We'll keep an eye out for him."

"He's big. Black. Pointed ears. Like a shepherd. Bigger. Thicker coat." He swallowed against the cracks in his voice.

"I'm so sorry."

Diego knees buckled. "He's gone to join his wild cousins."

"Pardon?"

"The vet warned me. I let him get away from me. And now he's gone."

Chapter 10: Visitation

Tara turned the wide brim of her hat around and around in her fingers. "I wish I had better news for you, Mr Sandoval. I really do."

She'd seen guys upset over losing dogs before but this man was crushed flat. Good-looking, in a young Antonio Banderas kind of way. At least he probably cleaned up nice when he showered and shaved and got some sleep. He sat on the top porch step and held the collar in both hands, staring at it as if it might talk to him.

"He must have been something special, eh?"

His brittle laugh made her cringe. *Any second now, he'll fall apart.* He surprised her, though, answering in a gentle, steady tone.

"Special, yes. That's a good way to put it. Thank you. For bringing it out to me."

"No trouble at all. I was up this way.

Like I said, we'll all keep an eye out. Ask visitors if they've seen him."

"I appreciate that."

"You going to be here for a few days yet, Mr Sandoval?"

He nodded, eyes on the collar again. "I… probably. I'll call you when I decide to go back home."

Tara climbed into her jeep and drove off, her heart aching for the dejected figure on the steps, dwarfed by that enormous house.

* * * *

"It's not as if he was a tame lion," Diego whispered to his reflection in the window. The line from the children's book failed to comfort him, though.

I should pack up and go home.

He didn't. He delayed another day and another. The weather looked threatening. He didn't feel well. Finn might come back. He couldn't disappear without saying goodbye.

The book still hung over his head, so he tried his best to forge on, Finn's taped voice both a comfort and a torment.

Chapter 7 Relationships

Your liaisons with humans all seem to have been short ones. A night or two at most. Haven't you ever had longer affairs?

"With humans? Yes."

And?

"I truly don't want to discuss it. Could we talk about something else? Anything else?"

How about relations with non-humans?

"Oh, well, those can't be

helped. When one is a duck in the springtime and approached by an amorous female..."

Um, I didn't mean that. Other intelligent beings.

"*Ducks are far from stupid.*"

(The long pause on the tape is me counting to ten.)

Other magical beings, I meant.

"*Why didn't you say so, then? Merciful currents, how am I to glean your meaning when you're so circuitous? Yes, from time to time one of the sidhe would catch my eye, or a merrow. There was a silkie off the southern coast who would swim upriver in the summers to guest with me. She was quite* lovely. Silken hair and silver-shimmer skin. And the way she wrapped her..."

(Thistle rhapsodizes at some length about the silkie's talents.)

"I've embarrassed you somehow."

No, not at all.

"Ah. You often turn such a fascinating shade of crimson."

Fine, maybe a little.

"So I shouldn't tell you about the five mer-siblings I had in one night?"

All at once?

"Interesting thought, but no. Mind you, I was a wee bit tired in the morning."

I bet. But if you're sleeping with multiple partners,

don't some get jealous?

"Sleeping with? That would be one of those odd things you say when you mean something else, wouldn't it? A... what's the word... a euphemism. No one was sleeping, bucko."

You know what I meant.

"Are you quite well? You're nearly purple now. Truly, I don't quite understand it but, yes, some of the sidhe can be territorial regarding their lovers. One found me entwined in her husband's arms. Enraged, she encased me in a prison of hardened swamp mud until I begged her pardon to her satisfaction. Dreadful stench, stayed in my nostrils for weeks. You would think I'd devoured her *children, the way she ranted."*

* * * *

Diego slumped on the porch steps staring at the coffee he couldn't drink. The empty black space lodged under his heart threatened to engulf him. He might have felt better if he could have mustered some anger. Good, solid, justified anger. But how could he be angry with someone for whom constancy and fidelity were foreign concepts? How could he justify even a moment's annoyance when he had repeatedly pushed Finn away?

I'm a damned fool.

He'd sunk so far into brooding, the irritating sound didn't register as the phone until the seventh or eighth ring. He cleared his throat twice before he could force out a hello.

"Diego? You sound like hell."

"Miriam. I'm not… feeling very well."

"You had a seizure last night?"

"No, nothing like that."

During the pause, he could picture Miriam's frown.

"Oh, shit, sweetie. Did you lose another one?"

"Excuse me?"

"Finn. Has he left you?"

"Can we keep this professional today, please? I can't handle anything else right now."

"'K, sorry. I emailed a contract offer to you. If you're good with it, send me a thumb's up and I'll Fedex the docs to you to sign. It's a fair deal, kiddo, but you let me know if it's enough."

"All right."

"Your first book deal and that's the best you can manage," she muttered. "You need me to come up there?"

"No. Miriam. Look, I'm... I'm so sorry. Thank you. Really. I'll jump up and down and holler and whoop when I feel better."

"Promise?"

"Promise."

He closed his eyes as he hung up the phone and tried to muster some spark of triumph or joy. Nothing.

"I have to go home," he told his ghastly reflection.

Home, where people needed him. Home, where all the sounds had names and the nights were never half so dark.

Home, where the oppressive silence of his empty apartment waited for him.

With the afternoon well underway, he couldn't start for home until morning. He packed instead, trying not to think about each thing Finn had worn or touched. His eyes stung when he picked up Finn's sneakers. Those beautiful feet. Maybe he should leave Finn's clothes, just in case. And the food in the fridge. He'd leave that out, too. Someone would eat it out in the woods.

That evening he gagged down a piece of dry toast, sat down to read the offer, and choked on his water when he reached the proposed figures. A fair deal, Miriam had said. For him, the sum represented a king's ransom, a nice parcel of isolated land and a comfortable cottage's worth. Without Finn.

He buried his head in his hands and wished he could cry.

* * * *

Three-quarters full, the moon glared at Diego through the front room windows. *Why are you still here*, it seemed to say. *You're an idiot twice over because you never belonged here or with him in the first place.*

He entertained thoughts of suicide. In a purely theatrical sense since he could never carry through with it, but the morbid scenes persisted. Park Rangers arriving days too late to find his body stretched out on the front steps in a pool of dried blood, flies buzzing around his sightless eyes. Finn's return greeted by the dry sound of his feet scraping the side of the kitchen stool he'd stepped from, his body swinging in a slow circle from the rope tied to the rafters.

There were practical issues, of course. He didn't own a gun and wouldn't know how to use one. The thought of slitting his wrists and leaving all that blood for someone else to clean up made him ill. The ceilings were too high here for him to reach the rafters, and he didn't think the ceiling fan in the kitchen would support a man's weight.

Most of all, his father had been through enough and how would his sister explain to her children that Tio Diego had committed such a cowardly act?

A scratch at the door jerked him from his brooding. He stood in the dark, heart pounding, and listened. There. Another hissing scratch, as of fingernails drawn across the wood. He held his breath and eased toward the door, not certain why he tried to walk so quietly. Probably a raccoon or a few leaves.

He flipped on the houselights, porch, side spot, and garage. A hasty scrabbling followed, and the retreat of heavy feet down the front steps. Two feet, not four.

"Finn?" The word escaped as a whisper. But Finn would have said something, wouldn't he? Something terrible must have happened. Hurt and frightened, he might not be able to speak.

Diego's hand trembled on the doorknob. Gripped by unreasoning fear, he stood paralyzed. What if it was someone else? Something else? But, dammit, he couldn't let Finn slip away again.

With a low sound in his throat, he rushed to the fireplace, grabbed the tongs, and flung open the door. The porch stood empty. He took a step out. The tongs rattled in his shaky grip. He reached back and eased the door shut behind him.

"Anyone out here?"

The wind whipped in a sudden gust, its voice through the porch columns a bestial moan. Movement caught the edge of his vision and Diego spun to his left toward the garage. A pale, naked figure stood just outside the circle of light, staring up at him. Wild, ebony hair twitched in the wind.

"*Dios*. Finn." Diego's lungs restarted and he held a hand out at he walked, one careful step at a time, toward the garage. "Stay there, please. Don't move. I'll come to you. What's happened? Are you hurt? Finn? Talk to me…"

He placed the fire tongs on the grass, realizing belatedly how threatening they would look. Finn made no movement toward him, or away, as he edged closer. The sense of something profoundly wrong escalated with each step. Finn's skin stretched taut across too prominent bones. Dark patches mottled his arms and chest. His eyes, half hidden under his matted hair, stared unblinking from sunken hollows.

Diego stopped out of arms' reach. "Give me something here, Finn. Anything. You're scaring the hell out of me."

Finn's lips stretched into a chill smile, exposing yellow, pitted teeth. Diego staggered back when a wall of carrion stench slammed into him.

Oh, God, not Finn. This thing is not Finn...

The thing's mouth never moved from its obscene leer, but as the wind rose, saturated with the stench of decay, it whispered his name.

His limbs leaden and trembling, he stumbled back another step. He had to get away, to run, but his legs wouldn't obey.

A shrill scream ripped the air, far from human. He jerked his head around toward the trees. Blacker than the shadows, a huge horse erupted from the woods. Rider-less, sparks flew with every strike of its hooves on stone. Its eyes blazed crimson flame as it bore down on him. Caught between nightmare and nightmare, Diego lost the ability to move in any direction.

A thousand tortured voices shrieked on the wind. The Finn-thing's mouth stretched farther, opening wide enough to swallow his head, as if its jaws unhinged like a serpent's. With an impossible leap, it sprang upon him and seized his arms.

The night shattered into a thousand jagged splinters.

Chapter 11: Awakening

Warmth on his face. Sun. Too bright.

Diego rolled away from the light with a groan. Small construction crews had set up worksites in his head, complete with jackhammers and excavators. Fire skewers shot through his back and limbs with every small movement.

The worst seizure yet, he'd never had one preceded by such evil hallucinations before.

He opened one eye and found himself on the ottoman in his clothes from the night before. He must have crawled there, though he couldn't remember. Arms wrapped around his head, he fought against nausea and self-pity. His own fault for not taking his meds. But it would have been nice to have someone there to take care of him. He eased his feet onto the floor and tried to convince himself to go to the kitchen for aspirin and tea. If necessary, he could crawl. He'd done it before.

"Good morning, my hero. How do you fare?"

The deep voice stopped his heart and sent it racing again. "Finn?"

"It's Finn. Original and unaltered. Accept no substitutions." Finn smiled as he repeated Rodney's formula. He stood hipshot in his black jeans, regarding Diego with his head cocked to one side.

The casual greeting, after all his anguish and doubt, infuriated Diego. Despite the pain, he staggered up and stalked over to straight-arm Finn against the wall. "Where the hell have you been?"

Finn's smile slipped. "Outside. Making certain the house is secure."

"No, not just now! Where've you been so long? Without so much as stopping in to say you were all right?"

"Diego… I haven't been gone so terribly

long." Finn appeared genuinely confused.

"Five whole fucking days! Without one damn word. Maybe that's not long to someone who lives forever but it is to me. I've been falling apart here thinking you were hurt or you'd died or I'd driven you away."

"I—" Finn closed his eyes and swallowed hard. He turned his gaze up to the ceiling and drew a long breath. "I have been a thrice cursed fool. I should have returned to you at the first sign of something odd. Never, never, you must believe me, did I wish to hurt you so."

He threw his arms around Diego in a crushing embrace. "And when I saw that thing had flown before me and arrived here first…oh, gods, I thought…"

Diego's legs turned to water as the room tilted. "You mean it wasn't a nightmare?"

"Yes. It is a nightmare. But that doesn't make it less real." Finn shifted his grip to lift Diego into his arms and cradle him against his chest. His face hardened as he carried Diego upstairs to lay him on the bed. "An ancient nightmare. Older than anything I have met before."

A thin, red line circled Finn's throat. Diego lifted a hand to trace along the mark. "You look terrible."

"My thanks, you are too kind."

"I mean you look exhausted. You don't even know how good it is to see you."

"And you." Finn caught the wandering hand and pressed Diego's fingertips to his lips. "Might I lie down with you?"

Diego scooted over to make room and held out his arms for Finn to fall into. "Are we safe?"

"For the moment. It does not like the sun and it cannot cross the threshold uninvited. So do not, under any circumstances, no matter whom it says it is or how hard it pleads, invite anything in. Especially after dark."

"What was it? What happened?" Diego repeated his earlier question gently. "Where have you been?"

"This is a story I would rather not have to share with you."

"You have to, Finn. I think that thing tried to eat me last night. You saved me?"

Finn's laugh sluiced over him like desert rain, a sound he thought he'd lost forever. "No, my hero. I tried my level best, but you saved yourself."

"What are you talking about? There was that rotting thing and that awful horse. I'm not sure which one scared me more. And all I did was collapse in a seizure."

Finn's forehead crinkled in a wounded expression. "That awful horse was me. Great mother of us all, now my day is complete. Not only did I bungle your rescue, I terrified you into a fit. I may as well fling myself into the sea and drown."

His mournful tone was so overdone, Diego couldn't help a laugh. "Sorry. You must have been as scared as I was."

"Ah, to see you smile again is worth a thousand wounds to my pride." Finn nestled closer, an arm wrapped around Diego's waist. "I was more so, I think, for I knew what you faced and you did not. But when it touched you, the lightning storms erupted in you. I think you hurt it somehow, for it shrieked and fled. Perhaps its touch caused the fit. I can't say."

"I don't suppose you'd start at the beginning for me?" Diego combed his fingers through Finn's hair, smoothing the thick mass over his shoulder. He stopped when he felt a flinch. Dark bruises marked Finn's wrists, and from his vantage point propped against the headboard, he could see the deep gashes across Finn's back, as if he had been raked by bear claws. Anger sparked in his gut. "It hurt you."

"'Tis naught but scratches."

"I need to take care of those for you." Diego tried to get up, prevented by Finn's arm.

"You'll do no such thing. You need to rest. As do I. What shall I bring you so you'll be content to lie still?"

Diego chewed on his bottom lip. "That little white bottle next to the coffeemaker. Some water. And a clean towel. Preferably not white."

"As you wish." Finn made a good show of sauntering off, though he stumbled twice on the stairs. When he returned with the aspirin, a bottle of water and a dark blue towel, he'd abandoned the pretense and had to catch himself on the doorframe.

"Take off those jeans and lie down before you take a header into the carpet."

"Are you quite certain you're Diego?"

"Why?"

"The one I know is forever after me to put clothes on."

"Just get over here. Face down." He

patted the bed beside him. When Finn had settled, he poured enough water out into the towel to start cleaning out the gashes, some only fingernail depth, others deep gouges. None bled any longer, but Finn must have left pints in the woods. From shoulders to calves, the slashes had been delivered with such precision, they almost appeared decorative.

"Must you do that? It hurts."

"I know they'll probably heal on their own while you sleep, but humor me, please. Let me feel useful." He hesitated over Finn's buttocks, those perfect, muscular globes he'd regarded with such longing. To distract himself, he went back to prodding Finn for information. "So you left me that day, ran into the woods, and then what?"

"I heard something."

"A voice? A twig snap? What?"

"No, in my head."

"You know, when humans hear things in

their heads, they're called crazy."

"Not like that. It's difficult to describe. But all beings give off a... mental scent, if you will. Each is unique. I could follow you by yours in the dark, provided there weren't too many other humans about. This feeling, this calling, came without a doubt from another magical being. Someone like me, Diego, when I thought I was alone. Imagine my excitement."

But you're not alone... Diego shoved aside the hurt. "Of course."

"I hared off after it, but it eluded me for a day and a night. I shifted from deer to wolf to raven, all the while believing myself the hunter. Ow!" Finn twitched and grabbed Diego's wrist. "I think there's a thorn in that one."

Diego nodded and bent over the back of Finn's thigh to retrieve the black point, acutely aware of Finn's scent and the feel of warm skin and hard muscles under his hands. Finn stretched, obviously enjoying the attention despite his complaints.

"Hunting." Diego cleared his throat against the husk in it. "You were talking about hunting."

"Hmm, yes," Finn murmured, eyes half closed. He drew in a deep breath and continued, without the light, teasing tone he usually used for his storytelling. "I was the prey, though I was too sure of myself to realize it. Led far away from the river, onto a place of tumbled stone, I should have been suspicious then, away from water and earth where I would be strongest. I called to it, resumed my own form, assured it that I wished only to speak with it."

He stopped to rub at his throat. "And walked directly into a noose snare. A carefully bespelled snare at that, rendering me unable to shift to free myself."

"It wanted to eat you, too?"

"I'd no idea what it wanted at first. I found myself beaten to my knees, my hands bound, and then I was hung upside-down. My attempts to plead with it seemed to confound it. Its attempts to communicate with me brought no clarity. I had only the vaguest impression of form at first—a chill being of wind, a dark hunger wrapped in unfathomable thoughts.

"At some point, it decided I would be more cooperative with a bit of pain applied. When it manifested..." Finn's hard shudder shook the bed. Diego lay down beside him again. "A huge shambling thing, half again as tall as me. Matted, reeking fur. Cadaverously thin with sunken yellow eyes. And claws a bear would have envied.

"Each time it raked me with those talons, it seemed to be asking something, but I couldn't comprehend what. And when the pain got it no farther than when it had started, the thing changed tactics. It forced its way inside my mind and began to rake through my thoughts and memories."

"God, how awful." Diego stroked the hair back from Finn's eyes, wanting to hold him, afraid of hurting him.

Finn took his hand. "At this point, I made perhaps my worst mistake. I tried to hide you, bundling all thought of you into what I hoped was a secure place. The more barriers I threw up, though, the more it knew that what I hid was what it wanted.

"Gods but it was strong. And I was... fading. It was like being besieged by a hurricane. Every obstacle I created, it ripped to shreds. And then it..." Finn's voice cracked. "I'm so sorry. I don't know what else I could have done. It found you. And once it had, it wanted you with a consuming avarice I've never felt before."

"But it failed. It didn't eat me."

"It doesn't wish to eat you, my hero. It does eat human flesh, yes. But you, it wishes to possess."

Diego felt those awful hands on his arms again and a wave of uncontrolled shivers hit him. "What exactly does that mean?"

"It saw the light you carry, saw the city full of people that is your home, and all those who trust you there. It wishes to inhabit you. To use your face, your form, your voice to lure its victims. I think it has avoided large human settlements and their machines out of fear. But with you, it sees a way to a hunting ground so vast and rich…"

Diego turned this over, fighting nausea. "And what would happen to me?"

Finn grabbed the front of his t-shirt in both fists and buried his head against Diego's chest.

"All right, we'll talk about it later." Alarmed by Finn's shaking, he wrapped his arms tight around him, cuts and all. "We can't solve anything in the state we're in now."

"I'm so tired," Finn whispered.

"I know. Close your eyes. Go to sleep. I'm glad you're home."

* * * *

"How long have you been up?" Diego's heart stuttered and lurched from waking up alone again.

"Not long."

"Cold?"

"A mite, yes."

Finn sat in the kitchen hunched under a blanket. Papers littered the table, covered in crayon-rendered, anguished shapes of black, gray and red with the occasional streaks of sickly yellow-green.

"This isn't your fault." Diego eased into the chair next to him.

"It most certainly is."

"How were you to know what would happen?"

A steady tearing punctuated the long pause as Finn peeled off his black crayon's paper until it lay naked and shining in his palm.

"I should have guessed its nature. Should have been more cautious in my approach."

"Cautious? I'm not sure who I'm talking to right now."

Finn slammed both fists against the table. "I should have been able to protect you! All the power at my fingertips, all the centuries of experience, and what good does it do? Not one cursed grain."

Your pride isn't wounded, it's shattered.

"There's always something stronger out there. That shouldn't be such a shock." Diego kept his voice flat and even, afraid Finn might fly apart with any show of sympathy.

"I woke it. My presence. The songs in my blood. It has slept long and deeply from what I could glean, and might have slept forever had I not come here. My reckless foolishness has imperiled you."

"And maybe not. Maybe it was ready to wake up anyway." He rubbed at his temples. "What do you want me to do with this little display? Hit you? Scream at you? Toss you out and tell you I never want to see you again? Stop feeling sorry for yourself. We have thinking to do."

Finn's hair obscured most of his face; Diego waited to see if he'd made matters worse.

"How can you be so calm?" The choked whisper barely reached him.

He took Finn's face between his hands, lifted his head and placed a soft kiss on his lips. "I'm scared to death. But I have you with me. Nothing's quite so bad now."

Under different circumstances, Finn's shocked expression would have been hilarious.

"You kissed me."

"I did. Need another?"

"Please."

Stiff surprise yielded to eager warmth the second time their lips met. Finn's soft moan sent a frisson of need through Diego's core. He disengaged Finn's fingers from the blanket and pushed the flannel back, baring him to the waist.

"Diego, are you certain? You said you didn't want—"

"Never mind what I said," he murmured against Finn's jaw, lips tracing a soft line down to the base of his throat.

"But if—"

"Sh. I was an idiot. Waiting for the perfect time. The perfect circumstances." Finn's head fell back as he licked along his collarbone. "Now is what we have. I'm not wasting any more of it."

"I simply don't want—"

"Kindly shut up, *cariño*, and make love to me."

"As you will."

Finn snagged the bottom hem of Diego's

t-shirt and pulled it off over his head. The simple slide of cloth over skin sent hard shivers through him. His breath caught when Finn's hands settled at his waist, the touch of his palms like sunlight on his skin. With a gentle tug, Finn urged him to stand, and then sank to his knees at Diego's feet. He rested his cheek against Diego's stomach, long arms wrapped around his thighs.

"I wanted you from the first moment I saw you. You were so beautiful, arriving at the moment of my bleakest despair." He caught Diego's hand and suckled on his fingertips.

"You don't have to say things like that." Diego combed his fingers back through the mass of shining blue-black hair.

"I only say what is simple truth. If I could but show you how you appear to me, your true form, as a radiant beacon in a darkened world... Even your own kind, blind as they are, are drawn to you. Why do you think the discarded ones trust you so?"

"Because I treat them like people instead of garbage." But as he gazed down into Finn's eyes, he wondered if there was more to it. Where the charity and social workers often failed to connect, with all their training and experience, he often succeeded. "I wish I could see as you do. Might make life easier to see someone's character as clearly as their face. But didn't you promise to shut up?"

"I made no promises." Finn shot him a crooked grin and leaned forward to press his tongue into the hollow of Diego's navel. "Though perhaps I could find better occupation for my mouth."

He took up a corner of the blanket to undo Diego's jeans, careful to keep the flannel between his skin and the steel zipper pull. Diego tangled his fingers into Finn's hair to steady himself. Too long denied, he felt as if the first touch might send him over.

Finn took his time. He tugged the jeans

down to Diego's ankles and left the boxers in place. A gasp leaped up from Diego's chest when he pressed his cheek against the iron hard erection tenting the cotton. Every muscle held taut, he fought to stay still, oversensitive nerves sending spider feet down his back. Finn stayed where he was until Diego relaxed, and then pushed at him in gentle nuzzles.

When Diego allowed a soft moan to escape, Finn snagged the elastic with his teeth and pulled the boxers down just far enough to settle the waistband under his balls.

"*Dios*… Finn… I won't last long. Oh. Damn." Both hands tangled in Finn's hair as his tongue caressed the tip. Finn's lips closed around him and slid down his cock by slow degrees. Diego's legs shook with the intense pleasure. "So sweet. Your mouth… I can't…"

Finn lifted his head. "Let it go, my hero. You need this. Give me what I so crave, to hear you sing for me."

He returned his mouth to Diego and plunged downward, taking all of his length. Soft sounds of pleasure followed faster now as Finn relaxed and let the tip slide past the tight constriction of his throat. His tongue traced the veins, curling all the way around in an impossible, prehensile way, holding Diego tight even as the suction increased.

The wonders of having a non-human lover… The sudden rush of tightening pressure in his balls cut off his speculation. He thrust his hips forward into that incredible mouth and clutched Finn's head tight. The soaring climb toward ecstasy tore a series of desperate cries from him. Finn wrapped his arms tight around his buttocks and he exploded, the hard pulses ricocheting up from his balls. His hips bucked hard until the spasms slowed, the room tilting in a strange, rocking motion.

Finn had him in his arms now, held him on his lap. "There, my love. Much better. Next time we shall proceed more slowly. But we had to take the jagged edges off you first."

He nuzzled at Finn's throat, unable to find the words for what he felt. Instead, he let his actions speak for him as nuzzles turned into soft kisses. Finn raised his chin so he could place sucking kisses along the length of his long, pale throat.

"Diego," Finn whispered, his trembling telegraphing how keyed up he was. "You needn't feel you must."

"But I want to. I need to." He slid down onto the floor to let his head rest in Finn's lap while he stroked his fingertips along the length of hard, pale shaft presented to him. "I want to taste you."

He rolled his thumb over the tip, spreading the pearl drops already waiting for him. His first taste made him moan. Finn's clean scent mingled with a taste so different from human males, sweet and cool, with undertones of mint and basil. He plunged down on Finn's cock in a desperate quest for more.

Finn shivered and gripped Diego's shoulders, his hips rolling gently rather than thrusting. "Such heat," he murmured. "Like plunging into the sun. Gods."

His hands slid into Diego's hair, encouraging him in his efforts. The taste grew sweeter as Finn's excitement mounted, his breaths coming in sharp gasps and little breathy moans.

He won't last long either, but then, seven hundred years is a hellishly long dry spell.

"Oh, my love, I'm—" Finn's warning came too slow, too late. Not that Diego minded. He clamped his lips around him to milk every last pulse, the taste of his seed a heady, spicy nectar he would be able to pick out of a thousand other flavors. With a pleased hum, he eased off slowly as Finn's shaft began to soften in his mouth.

Finn collapsed onto his back with a gusty sigh.

"Was it worth the wait?" Diego asked, his head resting on Finn's stomach.

"Beyond even the smallest grain of doubt."

Chapter 12: Besieged

The phone shrieked. Eyes still closed, Diego tried to reach over Finn to grab it, and nearly fell out of bed when he rolled into an empty spot.

"Thorpe residence," Finn said nearby. "Yes. Just a moment, I'll see if he's available."

Diego blinked the room into focus. Finn held the receiver out to him.

"The woman says she wishes to speak with you."

"Miriam?"

"So she said."

"Where did you learn to answer the phone like that?"

Finn's forehead creased in a worried frown. "From the picture box. Was it not the correct way?"

"It was perfect. Much better than most people." He scooted up to lean against the headboard and took the phone. "Miriam?"

"Is that him, kiddo? Is he back? Is that Finn?" Miriam spat out in a breathless rush.

Finn stretched back out on the bed, his head in Diego's lap.

"That's Finn. He came back last night." Diego couldn't keep the smile from his voice.

"Holy crap! That's got to be the sexiest goddamn voice I've ever heard!"

Diego held the phone away until her voice returned to a normal pitch.

"No wonder you were so torn up. I was just calling to see if you were okay. Ha! From the sleepy, I-got-me-some sound of your voice, you're more than okay, hon."

He stroked Finn's hair over his shoulder. The gashes on his back had closed while they slept. "I'm better. I did seize last night, but Finn was here." He couldn't even imagine telling Miriam the rest. She'd have him institutionalized.

"You tell him from me not to be such a shit and leave you hanging again. He'd better take good care of you to make up for it."

"He is. Thanks, Miriam."

"For what?"

"For worrying about me."

She snorted. "I've finally got you to the place where you can make me some money. Damn straight I'm gonna worry about you."

He laughed and reassured her once again that all was well before he hung up.

The warmth of Finn's body tempted him back under the blankets, but the latest horrifying twist of reality had to be faced.

"Put something on for me, *cariño*, please, so you're not quite so distracting." He stroked Finn's shoulder, his palm itching for more. "We have to get up and try to figure out what we're dealing with here."

Four-fifteen. Not much time before dark. Diego grunted as he swung his legs out of bed, still sore and stiff. Finn's arms wrapped around him immediately to help him up.

"I can still walk, you know. I'm tired, not crippled."

Finn backed off a step, hands spread. "Ah, well. I was merely finding excuses to hold you. Now that I'm permitted."

"Holding me is fine. No, strike that, it's wonderful." He raised his face to give Finn a soft kiss. "But you can't carry me around everywhere like some lost baby bird you found on the ground."

The smile slipped. "I would carry you for the rest of your life if you had the need."

Diego gazed into those black eyes and swallowed hard. What could he possibly say to that? "Hopefully, that won't ever be necessary." *Dios*. That was the best he could come up with? He patted Finn's chest and stepped around him. "Come down to the computer. Let's see what we can puzzle out."

When Finn arrived in the study, he'd pulled on his black jeans and a black t-shirt tight enough to outline every hard muscle in his torso. Naked would have been less distracting.

"Okay." Diego cleared his throat. "You said this thing can't cross the threshold. How do you know that for sure?"

"If it could, my hero, it would have done so last evening. Instead, it lured you away from the house. With my likeness. And a pretty bloody poor imitation at that, I might add." Finn slumped into the recliner in the corner. "Even if it had not done this, it is a magical creature and must abide by certain rules."

"That doesn't make any sense. You've never had a problem crossing a human-built threshold."

"Think for a moment. I have always crossed thresholds for the first time with you. With your arm about me, with your hand on my shoulder. With your touch, I have crossed.

Though the simple statement 'come in' would have sufficed as well."

Diego opened his mouth to protest and shut it again. He was right. At his own apartment, at the clinic, the museum, this house—every first time across, his hand had been in contact with Finn's body.

"So if it had stayed by the door and I thought it was you, hurt and sick, I would have…" Diego stopped and closed his eyes, forcing down the nausea.

"But it did not and you did not. No need to burrow into such dreadful thoughts."

"What about other entrances? Windows? Chimney?"

Finn shook his head. "If it had some powerful magic that would allow such things, it would simply have done so. No, inside we are safe. And trapped."

"But if it sleeps during the day, we could simply pack up and go. Tomorrow, when I feel up to driving. We'll go home…"

"It would follow." Finn slumped farther in his chair. "Your vehicle is swift but it cannot outrace the wind."

"Oh." The thought of leading that thing to a city full of people, where it could hide in dumpsters and sewers and feed at will on the homeless… He shuddered and turned to the screen to search for man-eating mythical creatures.

"I don't suppose you know what it's called? Or if it called itself anything?"

"I have only an impression of a sound. Something whispered in the chill. Witiku? Widigu? Something like it."

Diego felt the blood drain from his face. "Wendigo."

"Yes, something very much like that. It—Diego?"

He didn't answer, fingers flying over the keyboard as he waded through search engine findings, discarding the obviously questionable—B-movies, horror novels, sites written so badly a four-year-old might have posted them. A couple of university sites, postings from Native American studies departments, and an Algonquin Heritage site provided more plausible information. Even these accounts proved sketchy and contradictory except on two points: the wendigo was a creature of wind and ice, and it was indisputably malevolent.

"Diego?"

The hand on his shoulder made him twitch.

"You're white as frost."

"Sorry… sorry… It's just, if you were going to wake a mythical creature, couldn't you have disturbed a rabbit spirit or something?"

"I'll endeavor to be more selective next time," Finn murmured as he sank down at Diego's feet. "What does the writing box tell

you?"

"Nothing definite about how to get rid of it, unfortunately." He tried a search with 'exorcism' with no better results. "It's definitely a shapeshifter, like you—"

"Not like me." Finn sniffed in offense.

"I was going to say, 'in a much more limited way' if you'd let me finish."

"Your pardon."

"The stories talk about three types of manifestations. The first is the malevolent presence on the wind you felt. The second is human. Or rather, when it takes possession of a human. Wendigo-psychosis, it's called sometimes. And the third is a huge, shambling, hominid form, anywhere from eight to twenty feet high. Accounts are a bit vague."

Finn rested his head in Diego's lap. "It was monstrous. Hard to determine when one is hanging head down. But I wouldn't venture to say it reached treetop height."

"Small favors, I suppose," Diego murmured, scanning yet another site. "There's an odd remedy mentioned here, pouring hot wax down its throat to melt its ice heart. I only see that once, though, so I doubt it's accurate. Getting close enough to find out, I think, would be suicide. The only other way..." He stopped to lean back in his chair.

"Tell me, Diego!" Finn rose on his knees to take his face between his hands. "Whatever the price, tell me! I'll do anything to rid you of this fell beast."

"You wait until it possesses a human body." Diego swallowed hard. "Then you strangle the victim and burn the corpse."

"Ah." Finn subsided back to the floor. "Almost anything."

Diego stared at the screen without seeing it. "Finn..." He reached over to squeeze Finn's shoulder. "If it does manage to... take what it wants, I need you to make me a promise."

"You can't ask this of me."

"I know it's horrible, but what else could we do? If it possesses me, you have to kill me. You can't leave me trapped, living in that thing's head, watching it murder people and devour them."

"I'll…" Finn jerked away from him and paced to the far side of the room. He scrubbed a hand over the back of his neck, shoulders hunched. "If I can find no other way, if I truly have no other choice, I will end your torment. My solemn promise." He whirled back around, eyes blazing. "But there is always another way. I will not lose you. Not like that."

Hands clasped behind his back, he paced the room. "We will listen and watch. It will give something away as it grows more desperate. It will… Diego, where are you going?"

"It's getting dark. I want to make sure all the doors and windows are locked."

"I have told you and told you…" Finn

turned him and traced a finger along his nose. "It cannot come in."

"I know. But it'll make me feel better."

Finn helped him check the locks without any further protest. They finished in the great room, and Diego pulled the heavy drapes shut for good measure. He was trying to decide if he should suggest they have some dinner when Finn's head jerked up, nostrils flared.

"It's here."

The scratch at the door sent an ice spike through Diego's heart. He turned on all the outside lights as he had before but there were no retreating footsteps this time. The scratching persisted, followed by a soft whimpering.

"Maybe it's just a dog."

"No." One corner of Finn's mouth twitched up in a bitter smile. "No, I can feel it. I hear it. It is cold hunger and yearning. Oh, gods…" Finn wrapped his arms around his middle and sank into a crouch. "So empty… the agony of such emptiness..."

"Don't listen to it." Diego knelt beside him to hold him tight. "Can't you shut it out?" The door thumped against the deadbolt as the scratching grew to a scraping of heavy claws on wood. "What if it claws through the door?"

A sudden wind picked up and howled around the house, rattling the windows and thumping against the walls. The temperature inside the house plunged. Diego clutched Finn closer to share his heat.

"For the last time," Finn spoke through his teeth, as if the effort caused him pain. "It. Can. Not. Come. In." He took Diego's upper arms and set him back. Something odd shone in his eyes. "Watch."

"Finn, what..."

He rose, stalked to the door and flung it open.

"No! Finn, don't!"

The wind slammed through the doorway,

forcing Finn back a step. He steadied and faced the dark, arms flung wide. "Here I am! You wish to destroy me? All that stands in the way of your triumph? Then do your worst!"

"Finn! Close the damn door!"

The wind subsided. The sudden quiet sent chills up Diego's spine. From the front of the house, an eerie howl split the air, a sound filled with frustrated rage.

"You see, my love?" Finn turned his head to give Diego a grin. "It ca—"

A ferocious gust smashed into him and slammed him into the far wall.

"Finn!"

The gale howled through the house, toppling chairs and knocking pictures from hooks. Diego crawled, low to the floor, every breath a ragged gasp against the force of the wind. By slow degrees, he gained the door, wedged himself between it and the wall, and pushed with everything he had. Feet braced against the wall, muscles burning from the effort, he gained an inch and then another. A splintering crash sounded at the back of the house; he hoped a vase and not a window. His back screamed in agony, but he forged on against the tempest. Another inch, and another. He felt the door hit the sill, the wind inside the house abruptly cut off. With a last, desperate effort, he heaved the door shut. A relieved sob escaped him to hear the latch click and he scrabbled up the door to flip the deadbolt shut as well.

He crawled to Finn, trying to ignore the hurricane fury of the wind outside. Frost rimmed his hands and he trembled with chill. Finn slumped against the wall, pale and still. Diego couldn't trust himself to feel a pulse, his hands shook too much. He laid his head against Finn's chest. The solid thud of a heartbeat against his ear let him release the breath he'd held.

Finn's lids fluttered and soon those dark eyes found him.

"Dammit, Finn, what kind of a stupid, macho stunt was that?"

The pooka gave him a triumphant grin. "It can't come in."

Chapter 13: Afterglow

Spring nights had been pleasantly cool up to this point; the thing outside plunged the house into deep winter. The wind had blown out the pilot light, so the heater wouldn't fire. Diego hurried upstairs to grab every blanket and down comforter from the bedrooms so he could wrap Finn up tight. *It can't come in, it can't come in,* he reminded himself over and over each time the unnatural wind crashed against a nearby window.

Finn lay shivering on the sofa, nursing a cracked rib and an aching skull, while Diego struggled to light a fire.

"Please, please don't do things like that." Diego perched on the cushion next to him. "It could have killed you."

Finn opened the blankets to invite him into the warmth. "Quite a bit more effort would be necessary to kill me. When one heals so quickly—"

"Yes, yes, I suppose you could have your head hanging half off and still survive. Don't expect me to be happy about having to watch." Diego relented and nestled close. "What if it had used a weapon instead of just wind? Can it handle iron?"

"I couldn't say." Finn looked away, brows drawn together.

"Right. We don't know enough. And I think you would certainly die if you had an iron arrow through your heart. Tell me I'm wrong."

"I... no, you are not."

"Then don't tempt fate. All right?"

Finn stared into the fire without answering. He stroked Diego's back, his gaze far away. "There must be a way. There is always a way," he whispered to the flames.

Diego let him think, grateful for the life in his arms. He felt so secure in Finn's embrace, he dozed off. The soft touch of lips on his startled him awake. Finn's leg lay over his, lean body pressed close enough that Diego could feel the hard press of an erection against his stomach.

"Maybe this isn't the best time," Diego murmured against insistent, gentle kisses. "You're hurt. We're both tired."

"I'm much better already." Finn's voice vibrated against his throat as his lips pressed against the pulse point. "And I believe someone said now is all we have and we must take advantage of it."

"Finn—" Diego broke off with a moan when Finn's hand slid under his shirt, long fingers pressing and pinching his nipple. The front windows rattled and creaked from the assault again. "I don't know if I can."

"Your scent says otherwise," Finn told him in a husky growl. He slid his hand under Diego's waistband to stroke along the top curve of his backside. "I will beg if you require it.

Grovel on the floor if it would please you."

"Um, no. Rather you didn't."

"Oh, good." Finn sighed in exaggerated relief. "I didn't relish the thought of leaving the blankets."

Despite the fear, or perhaps because of it, Diego's shaft stirred. He shivered as another howl ripped through the night and Finn pulled him closer.

"Damn the beast," Finn muttered. He took Diego's face between his hands and closed the distance between for a ravenous kiss. "This is the sacred dance, my hero. Life. We turn our backs to death. He has no power here."

Diego traced a finger over his smooth jaw. "'If after every tempest come such calms, may the winds blow till they have waken'd death.'"

"Ah, a recitation. You are a bard, after all." Finn's smile turned wicked. "But you think too much." He yanked Diego's shirt off over his head and curled forward to plant hard, sucking kisses on his throat.

A sweet ache spread through his groin to his knees. Diego tipped his head back, letting the balm of surrender wash over him. The sacred dance, yes... oh, yes. He eased Finn's fly open and reached inside to take him in hand. Uncut, unmarred by modern sensibilities, Diego's palm slid easily over the slick head of his erection. The soft moan against his throat sent sparks through his veins.

"You sure you're up to this?"

"Wsht, my sweet." Finn's voice came out a husky growl.

"But your head—"

"Hush." Finn surged up and rolled him underneath, his smile soft and hungry. "I expect you prefer being the sheath to the sword."

"I'm... flexible." He swallowed hard, fighting the ridiculous urge to say things like 'take me now'. "You don't like it, ah, rough, do

you?"

Finn leaned his head on his fist. "Do you?"

"Not really, no."

"You have enough pain." Finn kissed his eyelids, down soft. "I would not add to it." He pulled Diego's clothes off the rest of the way and caressed him in long, soothing strokes over his chest and arms.

"That feels so wonderful," Diego whispered. Heavenly warmth spread from Finn's fingers, muscles relaxing in places he hadn't realized were in knots. He slid his legs around Finn so his foot could caress up one long calf. The anxiety he often had with a new lover between his legs refused to surface. This felt right; no, it felt perfect.

Finn wriggled out of his jeans and dove under the blankets to nuzzle at Diego's sac and lick behind it. He bit his bottom lip, but still, a gasp and a soft moan escaped when Finn slid lower. *Dios*, that tongue…

This careful preparation was something Mitch had often skipped, and when he did, it was fingers and lube, never his tongue. Diego squirmed, panting, fingers curled into the thick waterfall of Finn's hair.

"Must you mention him even while we make love?" Finn's head came up, his tone aggrieved.

"But I didn't—" Had he said it out loud?

Finn snorted and returned to his earnest efforts. The prehensile tongue pushed up inside farther than Diego thought possible and tapped against that sweetest of spots. He gripped Finn's hair tighter as his hips bucked.

"God… Finn… stop… oh, please," he gasped out. "I won't last for you this way."

With a soft growl, Finn crawled up his body to settle atop him. He angled himself to Diego's entrance and pushed with a gentle roll of hips, soft, teasing nudges until his head slipped inside. "Pray don't torment yourself, my sweet, about such small things. Simply be, feel. My pleasure lies in yours. I devour every scrap of it."

Diego arched, fingers clutched on Finn's biceps. The shaft slid deeper inside, smoother, cooler than a human's, glorious how it filled him, stroked him, and edged him onward despite the constant counterpoint of howls and rattles.

Hands and lips traveled over skin with slowly increasing need and ferocity. Diego wrapped his legs around Finn's waist to pull him closer; Finn slid his arms underneath to do the same. The ache soon escalated to a wall of pressure. Trapped between their bodies, his erection throbbed with every slide of Finn's powerful body, every kiss which blazed across his throat and chest.

"Finn," Diego pulled back, panting. He wanted to watch Finn while he came. The request stuck in his throat. "Finn, you're... glowing."

Hardly the word, but his passion-muddled brain failed to find words to describe the colors dancing like a halo over Finn's head, around his body, under his skin. *Warm blue, how can blue be warm?*

His confused thoughts flew away in a flock-of-crows scatter as his orgasm slammed up through him in a sudden rush. "*Dios...* Finn..."

"Oh, my Taliesin," Finn whispered, as he heaved and bucked atop him, hips jerking as he came in hard, short thrusts. "You begin to heal, to touch the world again."

* * * *

Chapter 9 Magic

Thistle sits with me by a

stream. He feels most comfortable near or in water. At the moment, a globe of water hovers over his palm while the silt forms swimming fish shapes inside.

How do you do that?

"Do—Oh, well, there's not much to it. A small magic."

I couldn't do it.

"Perhaps if you were not so stubborn. You could try."

There's no magic in my fingers, not like yours.

(Thistle laughs and the water globe falls back into the stream.)

"Of course there is, bucko. You simply don't feel it. You don't feel the blood flowing through your veins, either. Not *unless there is some pounding pressure or pain, or if you bleed profusely. So it is with magic as it flows through you, around you, within every fiber of your being. Threads and flows and tendrils, cascades and cataracts and floods of it. It connects you to every other thing, every petal, every bird, every stone, every star, to every possibility, every lifetime, every word ever spoken. It is, you are, you have no less or more than I have."*

(He takes my hand and holds it palm down over the stream.)

"Here, while I speak to the water, coax it to me, do you feel it? Feel the dance of the water? The joy of its song?"

No. I'm sorry. I don't feel anything.

"Ah. Please forgive me. I forget how wounded and ill you have been."

* * * *

Only their gasping breaths broke the silence. The howls and shrieks had ceased.

"Is it gone?"

Finn sifted through the night a moment, still fogged from one of the most incredible orgasms in a thousand years. "It has retreated." He combed through Diego's hair and kissed his forehead. "Perhaps it was jealous."

"Maybe." Diego gave him that hesitant half-smile, the one that so tugged at his heart. "What was that? At the end? Was I seeing things or do you always, um, shine during sex?"

Small degrees, one had to lead Diego in

small degrees, his disbelief a greater barrier than any powerful spell. In the unguarded, heated moments of passion, though, he had heard his lover's thoughts clearly, as if he sent them with purpose. He murmured into Diego's shoulder while his member softened inside his heated sheath. "Your channels... open. Out here, away from the city. You begin to reach out with things long shuttered."

"And here I thought I was asking a yes or no question," Diego said on a soft sigh. "I don't even know what you mean."

"There are other ways to see beyond your eyes. Other ways to feel than with your hands."

"Magic, you mean."

"Even so, my hero."

Chapter 14: Finn's Stand

The crickets chirped outside the door again the next morning, reemerged from whatever place they hid during the unnatural storm. Finn still slept, curled cat-content on the sofa.

"The woods are lovely, dark and deep," Diego muttered as he sipped his coffee. Too bad Mr Frost had failed to understand the woods also held dire and terrible things. He stared out into the trees a moment more, longing for the simple days of sun-dappled trails and scrambling over roots and logs. "Promises to keep and so on."

He returned to his computer and his research. Some kernel of inspiration would appear; he desperately needed to believe it would. An hour into his largely fruitless search, Finn's soft tread padded down the hall.

He wrapped his arms about Diego's

neck. "Good morning. My arms were empty."

Diego turned his head to kiss a warm forearm, though he didn't take his eyes from the screen.

"Have you found aught, my hero? Some scrap or crumb to aid us?"

"Not much, I'm afraid. There is a story about a shaman who killed one."

"Shaman? What might that be?" Finn leaned forward to nuzzle at his ear.

"A healer, a person who spoke with the spirit world. I suppose kind of a wizard, though not one who tried to control nature. In this case, one of the original tribal people who lived here."

"Ah. A druid."

Diego turned his head to look at Finn and received a soft kiss. "Yes, like that."

"And how did this shaman defeat the beast?"

"It sounds like just a story to me. Talks about the shaman and the wendigo both becoming gigantic and raging back and forth across the forest. He wins, but it doesn't say how."

"Pity." Finn sank down to sit cross-legged on the floor, his head on Diego's thigh. "Do you know any shaman?"

"No."

For a few minutes, Finn picked at carpet threads in silence. "We should speak to the wisewoman. On the little far-speaker, the… phone. We could do this, yes?"

"Who are you talking about, *cariño*?" Diego murmured, only half listening.

"Tia Carmen."

"Oh. You think she's a…" Diego let the question trail off. The herbs, the calm acceptance, the little charms of bones and feathers in her apartment suddenly made him uncertain.

He called, and she answered on the second ring.

"*Tia Carmen, estás una bruja?*"

"*Sí, por supuesto,* Santiago. But why would you ask such a thing now? You have always known I believed in the old ways."

"Yes, but I always thought it was just old customs, old superstitions. I never thought of you as a... witch. Finn calls you the wisewoman."

"Your Finn has his eyes open. What's happened, *querido*? Something is not right, I think."

He told her everything without hesitation, things he would have thought insanity or at least fantastic lies a month before. She listened in silence without skepticism or questions.

"*Pobre niño*. I hoped you would have some peace up there," she said on a little sigh when he had finished.

"So did I."

"Does Finn know how to use the phone

now?"

"Yes, he's figured it out. Why?"

"Let me speak to him, please."

Diego hesitated in confusion, and then held out the phone. "Tia Carmen wants to talk to you."

"Ah, good." Finn took it. "Good morning, dear lady, how do you fare in that monstrous poisoned village?" He paused to listen. "Oh, yes. As you said. And it was wonderful. He's quite…"

His voice trailed off as he left the room for a more private conversation. Diego's ears burned; he didn't want to know.

Finn's voice soon grew louder and more agitated, though, impossible not to overhear. "Yes, yes, I thought of that! And so has he! I can't allow it—No, I know. There has to—Pardon? It might be. Perhaps."

His voice subsided and Diego lost his half of the conversation again. When Finn returned, the phone beeped its off-the-hook warning. "Take it, please, my hero. Gods. Why is it screaming at me? Have I hurt it?"

"No, you just need to learn to turn it off now." Diego did, but the absence of noise failed to ease Finn's anguished look. "What did she say?"

"Naught of any importance."

"Finn, please."

"She said such a terrible hunger creates a void in the universe and it must be filled. She says it is the only way to defeat the thing. I told her I cannot, by gods, I will not sacrifice you to the thing. She said she understood but nevertheless, the hunger, the empty place, must be filled." Finn flung himself down beside Diego, head in his hands.

"*Cariño*, don't get so upset." Diego stroked his hair. "Maybe she meant something else."

"What else? We hold the beast's mouth

open and pour sand in to fill it? There is no 'else'! And it will not have you!" Finn surged to his feet again and began to pace the house, muttering to himself.

After an hour, Diego intercepted him in the upstairs hall. "Stop. Just stop. All this stomping around is giving me a headache." He wrapped his arms around Finn and rested his head on his chest. "Come sit with me. Have something to eat. Hurling epithets at the problem doesn't seem to help you think any better."

Finn leaned his head on top of Diego's. "Your pardon, my love. I didn't mean to distress you."

"I'm not distressed. You're just making me crazy."

A plate of chicken salad and a long make-out session on the front porch later, Finn curled up in a patch of sunlight and went back to sleep.

"Must be nice," Diego murmured, with a little smile. If only all his lovers had been so easy to please. He went back inside to make the belated call to the ranger station to call off the search for his dog.

As evening approached, Finn seemed calmer. He sat at the kitchen table engrossed in a drawing of red and orange water-droplet globs. When Diego returned from his ritual of checking the doors and windows, Finn stood and took him by the shoulders.

"Wish me luck, my love," he said with a forced smile.

Diego's heart sank. "Why? What are you planning?"

"You make me sound devious," Finn protested, hand over his heart.

"Finn, don't—oh, God, please don't."

He pulled Diego into a fierce embrace. "I should have done this long since. Cowering here at night, instead of going out to face it. You have sheltered me and protected me from the first moment we met, my hero. Past time for me to return the favor. More than a favor. In this, it is my place to protect you."

"But the last time it got hold of you—"

"I was ambushed and snared. I go out to issue challenge, to stand and fight as I should have done in the first place."

Diego lifted a hand to smooth the silken strands of hair back from his face. "Don't be an idiot. This isn't some cheesy Western and it's not high noon. We'll find another way. I don't want you hurt. Or worse."

"Ah, he cares." Finn kissed his fingers. "But it would do my heart good to know you had a shred of confidence in me. It nears, Diego. Kiss me and tell me you love me."

"Finn, I—" The words stuck in Diego's throat. He wasn't going to talk Finn out of this. *Dear God, oh, dear God.*

"Well then." Finn's smile slipped a bit.

"Kiss me at least and be prepared to give me a hero's welcome on my return, eh?"

Long arms folded him close and Finn closed the distance between them, a lightning spark of heat in his kiss before he pulled back with a wink and a grin. He strode to the front door with Diego trailing like a dust mote in the wake of a hurricane.

"Finn!" He tried once more at the front door while anguish threatened to swallow him.

"Stay inside, my love," Finn demanded as he strode onto the porch. "I must know you are safe. No distractions. Stay back from the doors and windows."

The soft blue light danced over his skin as Finn spread his arms to the night. His form melted, grew, and resolved into a Kodiak-sized black bear.

"But you said it can't reach me inside," Diego protested, his voice far too small against the rising wind.

"It can't." The bear turned back to give his shoulder a pat. "I can't say the same for flying debris. Close the door. Do not open it, no matter what you hear. Not until the sun's orb clears those trees. Promise me. Swear it."

Diego swallowed hard, heartsick. No distractions. He had to give Finn that much of a chance. "I promise. *Lo juro.* Not until I see the sun over the trees."

Bear-Finn shambled down the porch steps and rose onto his hind legs. "It is here."

A piercing shriek shot through the rising howl of wind. Finn flung his head back and roared challenge.

"Oh… God… Finn," Diego whispered as he heaved the door shut. Through the front windows, the bear remained visible as he charged toward a huge dark shape lurching from the trees. Then the wind slammed full force into the glass. The casements rattled and creaked. Diego retreated to the upstairs hallway, one of the few windowless spots in the house.

He gathered comforters into a nest. The temperature would plummet soon. A heavy thud vibrated through the wall. Roars mixed with unearthly shrieks. The wind tore at the house until he wondered if the roof would fly off. Did the magical prohibition extend to the roof? If the house lay in ruins, did the threshold rule still hold?

And the wind did howl, and the wind did blow...

The song rose unbidden from his memory and he whispered the words as he rocked back and forth in his blankets. "Get down, get down, little Henry Lee, and stay all night with me..."

Something screamed and a terrible crash hit near the back wall.

"And the wind did roar and the wind did moan..."

His whispers rose to compete with the

bedlam outside as he ran through chorus and verses again and again, until his voice grew hoarse. A shivering splinter came from one of the back bedrooms, followed by the discordant notes of glass falling to the floor. Finn bellowed words he couldn't understand but the defiance rang clear, still on his feet and fighting.

Through the terrible sounds of battle, Diego concentrated on Finn, as if he could send strength to him. He imagined he could feel Finn's bright warmth against his mind. His own brain created the illusion to comfort him, no doubt, but he clung to it regardless.

A deafening crack sent him under the covers like a small child in a storm. "Dammit, Finn, why did you suddenly have to play Lancelot?" He huddled, shuddering through what seemed hours of violent cacophony.

When the noise finally ceased, it happened so abruptly he thought he had gone deaf. He crept to the top of the stairs, listening.

Was it over? And if it was, why didn't Finn burst through the door to tell him? Nothing, no sounds reached him at all besides his own breathing, the absence of sounds in the woods more ominous than any of the screeches and calls of a normal night.

He eased downstairs, every creak on the steps a gunshot in the silence. Wait; there was a sound now, the susurration of something dragging along the planks of the front porch. He pressed his ear to the door. The sound stopped directly in front of him.

"Finn?" he whispered.

Help me...

He wasn't certain if his ears heard the words or his mind. "Finn?"

Diego... help me...

He had promised. No matter what he heard, he would keep the door shut. But what if it was Finn? What if he was so badly hurt he couldn't speak, so badly wounded he wouldn't make it through the night?

His hand shook on the doorknob. "*Cariño*, if it's you, you'll have to figure out some way to let me know."

The porch light refused to turn on, the bulb most likely broken. Diego eased the door open a crack. The biting cold sent fire down his throat. A long, pale body lay stretched out on the planks.

"Say something," Diego urged in a desperate whisper. "Anything and I'll pull you inside."

The body shifted as if trying to rise; the head lifted to meet the light streaming from the house. Dark patches mottled a face hidden by wind-whipped hair. Diego stepped forward, straining to see. A long-fingered hand reached toward him.

"Close that thrice-cursed door!" Finn's voice bellowed from his right.

Diego startled back a step. The face in

front of him split in a sickening, cadaverous grin. *Not Finn, Dios, not Finn.* A roar shook the house. The wind rose to shriek through the doorway. The thing on the porch leaped up, Finn-shape melting into something huge and dreadful. Diego glimpsed a rush of enormous wings and a sinuous black shape that slammed into the wendigo before he wrestled the door shut.

"Ohgodohgod," he whispered, and sank down on the bottom step in the hall, heart slamming against his breastbone. 'Don't open the door, no matter what you hear,' Finn had said. He sat watching the grandfather clock's pendulum and the slow tick of its hands, waiting out the hours, desperate for the first gray hint of morning.

Chapter 15: Isis by Necessity

The first flame glints of sun pierced the filigree of branches. Silence had wrapped the house since two in the morning, the battle evidently over, but no sign of Finn.

Diego stared out the front window, shadows tugging and toying with his aching eyes. Crawling dread joined the leaden, nauseous sensation of sleep deprivation. His ability to reason might as well have leaked out his ears in the night.

Damn the stupid promise. I can't wait anymore.

The sun was nowhere near clearing the trees but enough light filtered through to see, he hoped enough to discourage nocturnal creatures.

He eased out into the mist-shrouded morning, eyes searching for any sign of a hulking shape lurking by the house or in the grass. Branches of every size littered the front lawn, blown down in the fierce winds or broken off by hurtling bodies. An ancient pine lay across the driveway, branches yearning skyward as if it struggled to rise.

"Explains one of the crashes, anyway," Diego murmured to the large cricket on the front step. "I don't suppose you're Finn?"

The cricket leaped away to hide in the grass.

"That would've been too easy."

When no shambling, reeking creature appeared and no cadaverous hand reached up over the porch planks, he ventured forward. Visions of every horror movie he had ever watched assailed him. This was the part where everyone in the audience would be yelling, 'Don't go out there, you idiot!' *Great. Reduced to a B-movie extra.*

"Finn?" he called in a soft, hoarse voice. When nothing stirred, he tried a little louder. No answer. He shivered in the unnatural quiet.

While he would never have claimed to be a tracker, there appeared to be a clear trail of crushed plants and broken limbs to show the path of the battle. He started toward the woods, trying to watch in every direction at once.

The whisper-splash of the little stream by the side of the house had just edged into his hearing when he tripped on something in the grass. Instinctively, he turned, felt around, and picked it up.

"God! Oh, shit!"

The dismembered hand fell from his numb fingers as he staggered back a step. Finn's hand confronted him like an accusation in the grass, the long fingers that had caressed him the night before contorted and blood spattered.

"No, oh, no… Finn!" Diego searched frantically through the high grass near the stream. Blood dotted the vegetation, darker than human. He said he could put himself back together, said it would take a lot more than—

His boot hit the body before he spotted it. He flung himself to his knees, hope draining from him when he gathered what was left of Finn up in his arms. His right leg lay twisted, bone protruding from the thigh, his right arm ended in a mangled stump, his left eye socket stared, black and empty, and a chunk of flesh had been ripped from his side.

A distant part of Diego told him he should be horrified and nauseated but his grief drowned out everything else.

"*Cariño... querido...*" he whispered. "Why did I let you go? *Dios...* oh... fuck... why didn't I tell you I loved you when I could?" He held Finn's maimed body close and rocked him. The tight bands around his heart snapped and a sob escaped, followed by a torrent of tears.

Ants had crawled onto Finn's hip. He brushed them away. A fly buzzed nearby and he shooed that off as well. A sparrow-sized black bird, probably a scavenger, sat in the grass nearby.

"Go away!" Diego shouted at it through heaving breaths. "Leave him alone!"

The little bird fluffed its feathers and opened its beak. "Honestly, my love, you do confound me, weeping over me with one breath and ordering me off with the next."

Diego blinked back his tears. "Finn?"

The bird gave a tired cheep. "No substitutions and all of that. Yes, it's me. I have been forced into a smaller vessel for the moment. I believe you can see the wisdom in that."

"You bastard." Diego wiped his sleeve over his eyes. "You let me sit here and bawl over you. I thought you were dead, dammit."

"I most humbly beg pardon. I had some difficulty gathering myself together this much to speak to you." The absurdity of Finn's deep voice issuing from such a tiny bird should have been hilarious, but the gray weariness of his tone ruined any possibility of humor.

Diego leaned over to pick Bird-Finn up in his palm, where he huddled, shivering. "*Caro*, I'm sorry. I shouldn't have snarled."

"Not to worry, my hero. I'm so pleased you're here that you could heap curses on me if you liked."

"Are you—never mind. Of course you're not all right. Is this..." Diego trailed off, struggling for words. "Fixable?"

"One hopes." The tiny bird cheeped again, in obvious pain. "Given a number of weeks I could manage on my own, perhaps. I would rather not take the time, though, so your help would be much appreciated."

"What can I do?"

Finn rubbed his feathered head against Diego's thumb. "I need you to play the part of a particular goddess for me. Ah, now, you must know the story, m'boy. The wife of that southern god, the one whose brother hacked him to pieces and scattered him across the land."

"Osiris?"

"The very one. Yes. So you must play lovely, grieving Isis for me and gather up the scattered bits."

"Oh." Diego took a deep breath, a bit of nausea creeping in. "You can't just spell yourself back together?"

"Now if I could have done it, do you think I would have let you find me in such a state? Sweet gods of water, Diego, think a moment."

"Sorry. And what do I do when I, um, have you in one place?"

"If you would place all the pieces in the streamlet over there, I will manage the rest. I don't require much water if it's clean."

Diego tucked the tiny body into the front of his jacket. "You know, if I had to go in legendary drag, I would've preferred someone else." He rose to retrieve the severed hand. "Penelope, maybe. Her man comes home safe and sound."

"My apologies for the necessity, my love," Finn murmured.

"Joke. That was a joke."

"Ah."

Diego picked up the major part of Finn's mass, husk light as if the flesh were no more than dandelion fluff without Finn inside. His stomach lurched to see the body he had so recently made love to flop gracelessly into the water.

"Steady, my hero. I am here," Finn reassured him, the deep voice vibrating against his chest. "The rest is merely the clay I work with."

"I'm OK. Just hard to look at." Diego moved away into the grass again so Finn could direct him to the next piece. "You want to tell me what happened?"

"Aside from me being ripped asunder?" Finn shifted about, getting comfortable. "The eye is there by your left foot. Ah, I am a great fool. The thing was much stronger than I could have imagined."

"You seemed to be holding your own when I saw you on the porch as a... what? A giant bat?"

"Dragon."

"Oh."

"There's a toe over there in front of you. Yes, at that point it still was more concerned with drawing you out of the house. But after you shut the door, it summoned the wind and cold with a vengeance. As if I battled an ice storm. It seemed everywhere and nowhere at times, insubstantial, yet solid enough to achieve what you see here. On your left, my love, a piece of ear."

With Finn's voice a constant presence, Diego was able to accomplish his grisly task, and soon had all the bits in a little pile in the stream. "Now what?"

"Now you place me in the water as well," Finn answered. "Gently... oh, dear gods, gently, if you please."

Diego withdrew his fingers to leave the tiny ball of feathers floating atop the water. Bird-Finn closed his eyes and vanished. Diego cried out in horror when the rest of the body parts melted into the stream as well. "Finn, no! Don't go!"

"Wsht, now. So little faith in me." Finn's voice floated up, muffled and distant from the streambed. "It will take some hours to heal far enough to reform, love. Go back to the house. Rest. I would wager you had no sleep last night."

"I don't want to leave you." Diego's chest hurt again, his eyes swimming. "I thought I'd lost you."

Finn was silent a moment, then he asked,

"Why is it humans so often wait until they believe it too late before they declare their love?"

Diego let out a strangled sob. "I don't know, I don't know. It's incredibly stupid. And I do love you."

"And I you, my hero. I am pleased that you cried over me."

"God, you're such a walking ego." Diego sniffed and wiped at his eyes.

A warm chuckle floated from the stream. "I meant it was good that you were finally able to cry again. You are less clouded now. Go back to the house, Diego. I will join you again when I am able to—what is the expression I have heard? Drag my sorry ass up there?"

Diego managed a cracked laugh. "All right. Tonight?"

"Most likely tomorrow, my love. This will take some time."

Chapter 16: One Step Too Far

Relieved and steadied, Diego returned to the house to assess the damage. Only one bedroom window had been shattered and only the one tree had come down. He had expected much worse.

"Miriam? I'm sorry, did I wake you?"

"Damn right you did, kiddo. Who the hell's up at this ungodly hour?" Miriam grumbled into the phone.

"Me, I suppose." Diego winced at the stream of soft curses, probably Miriam levering her bulk up to a sitting position. "Sorry, sorry. I just need some advice and I didn't want to wait until too late in the day. We had sort of a... freak windstorm last night. Broke one of the back windows and left a huge tree across the drive. Who should I call up here to take care of things like this?"

"You and Finn OK, sweetie?"

No, Finn's not. Know any good fairy surgeons? "Finn didn't have the best night but he'll be fine, don't worry. I just don't want to leave things like this since it's a little chilly at night."

"And I sent you up there to get away from the distractions." Miriam snorted. "Don't you worry your pretty head. I'll call Jake and tell him what happened. He'll take care of everything."

"Jake?"

"Handyman, lumberjack, tow truck slash snowplow driver. Typical for up there, to have one guy who can handle just about everything. You don't even have to be there. Just leave the door open for him."

"Leave the—Miriam, I can't go out and leave your door unlocked."

"It's Canada, sweetie. No one locks their doors."

Despite her reassurances, he stayed to

wait for Jake. The realization that their predicament might not have a solution spurred him to finish his manuscript. If he died because of this little jaunt into the woods, he wanted the book to live after him, his gift to Finn.

He settled down at the computer and shivered on a spider-feet crawl of chill up his back. With Finn piecing himself back together, he would have to face a night alone with the wendigo raging and howling around the house. Maybe more than one night if the process took longer than Finn anticipated, or more still if he slipped away in the Dreaming too far to be called back. Oh, yes, that was the last part.

Chapter 20: The Dreaming

Thistle decides one evening the white wall in the kitchen will make a good canvas.

Imagine my surprise when I wander in to find an abstract study in green and yellow in progress. This conversation takes place while I clean crayon off the wall.

"You're angry with me."

No, not really.

"You are. Your voice is soft but your forehead has that crease in the center and you won't look at me."

OK, maybe a little annoyed. But I never said you couldn't use the walls, so how would you know?

"I do wish humans could express themselves more clearly. A simple 'yes, what you did hurt me' would be much preferable to hidden grudges that lead to *unpleasant things."*

I'm not planning something dark and terrible; I'm cleaning the wall.

"Your pardon. Perhaps I should not include you in such statements. You do channel your anger somewhat differently."

Would you like to tell me what made you say it? Obviously someone hurt you.

"Yes, they did, and no, I'd rather not discuss it. I spent seven hundred years in the Dreaming trying to forget, and you want me to dredge it all up again?"

You've mentioned the Dreaming before. Is it like the Otherworld, the place across the Veil? Could you find your way back to the court that way?

Thistle laughs. "M'dear, you are so delightful in your ignorance at times."

So enlighten me.

"You mistake a planar shift with a state of mind. To cross the Veil is to be somewhere else. A place that shares the same sun and moon as this one, and exists in tandem with it, but is separate all the same. The Dreaming is simply another sort of consciousness. There is waking and sleeping and the Dreaming."

Oh. So you weren't asleep for seven hundred years?

"Not precisely, no. I wasn't awake either."

And I'm the one who's

supposed to be unclear.

"*Try to explain sleep to someone who has no inkling of what it is.*"

Good point.

Thistle gnaws on a sparerib bone while he thinks. "The Dreaming is a state of refuge. You wrap the magic tight around you, a shield against prying eyes and minds. It gives one time to heal, to re-weave oneself."

It's a place to hide.

"*No!*" *Thistle pulls his feet up onto the chair and rests his chin on his knees. "Yes. In dire straits and heartbreak. I never claimed to be terribly brave.*"

* * * *

Jake turned out to be cheerful, practical, and completely unperturbed by the passage of a half-acre wide windstorm.

"That's spring weather for you, eh? We get some weird stuff out here. Small tornado, probably." He shrugged and directed the two young men with him to get out the chainsaws. "Billy and Mick'll take care of the tree, Mr Sandoval, don't you worry. And I'll take care of the window. We're gonna be making an awful lot of noise, though, y'know. So if you wanna clear out for a bit, couldn't say I'd blame you."

"I'm going to make a run to the post office while you're busy," Diego offered. With the winding, uncertain roads, a 'run' to the post office could take two hours. "Do you need anything out that way?"

"Oh, no, thanks for askin', though. We'll be out of your hair by suppertime. Ms Thorpe says you need quiet so you can get some work done."

"Oh, did she?" Diego chuckled. "Such a slave driver."

Diego took the truck into the little gathering of houses and businesses that passed for a town and sent both signed contract and manuscript off to Miriam. He had ended with a couple of paragraphs on the last page cautioning the reader to keep an open mind when confronted with someone odd. *An inability to recognize common names or unfamiliarity with machinery may mean you have met one of the last of the fae rather than an eccentric psychiatric patient. Be kind, be patient, listen carefully, and you may hear secrets and dreams we humans lost long ago.*

He stopped at the little grocery for cream, eggs, and chamomile tea. If Finn did come back that evening, he might need to be coddled and fussed over.

When he returned to the house late that afternoon, Jake and his boys were cleaning up. They showed him the neatly stacked woodpile by the garage and the new window, then said their goodbyes. The huge trucks lumbering away into the woods seemed to Diego a last glimpse of companionship and civilization. The sun dropped below the tree line without any sign of Finn, and he braced himself for another long night.

* * * *

Shaman.

The chill voice yanked Diego from a light doze. He lay on the ottoman wrapped in blankets by the fire, since he didn't have any illusions about a good night's sleep. Had he dreamt it?

Shaman, come and see.

"I'm not going out there, you mangy

scavenger," he muttered, with more bravado than he felt. *Why is it calling me that?*

It called again and again, soft and coaxing, while the wind tugged at the house in little gusts and whistles.

"*Dios*," he whispered, and got up with the blankets wrapped around him. "What do you want?"

Dread gripped him, but the soft persistence compelled him to look. What if—no, Finn had said he would be hidden while he healed. He crept to the front window and peeled back a corner of the curtain.

The empty front porch stared back at him. With a slow exhale, he pulled the curtain open farther. Nothing, good, still nothing. A heavy object slammed against the glass. He staggered back with a sharp cry. The wendigo leered at him, inches from his face. He retreated another step. The glass between them suddenly did not seem enough.

Blood dripped from the thing's decay-riddled teeth. Glistening lumps decorated its matted fur. It wore its own face now rather than Finn's, more bear than human, but a bear that had been dead for some months.

"Go away," Diego whispered. "Please go away and leave us alone."

Look, Shaman. I have a she. You know this one.

The frigid, hollow thoughts pierced his head, scattering his wits. "You have…"

In answer, the wendigo held up its gruesome prize. A woman's mutilated body hung from its grip. A ragged, gnawed stump was all that remained of the right leg. The head still dangled from the neck by a few flaps of skin. It turned the body so the head flopped backward and Diego could see the face.

"Tara," he got out in a strangled whisper. "Oh… holy shit."

You are not pleased, Shaman. The

wendigo brought the body up to its face. It opened its mouth wide enough to unhinge its jaws and bit down to tear a chunk from Tara's side. Gobbets of flesh fell with nauseating, wet sounds onto the porch. *You do not wish for me to eat this one. The flesh is strange. The taste. Sharper. But the bones—*

It opened its maw again and bit down on Tara's ribcage. *The bones still snap and crunch.*

"Stop!" Diego shouted. "God... please stop!" Emptiness, such terrible emptiness filled his head with every thought, black, unceasing despair.

Join with me. Calm your lightning and let me touch you. Let me live in your skin. Then we will hunt together. You will help me choose which ones to eat.

"No, I can't! I can't eat my own kind! I can't kill for you!"

Hunt with me. Help me choose. Or I will choose another each night. One with your scent on them.

Diego's stomach lurched. Jake, Mick and Billy, the ladies at the post office and the grocery, the teenager at the gas station—they would all carry his scent. He would be their deaths. A sudden rush of anger swept through him, a forest fire of rage that rose from his belly to his head.

"*Hijo de puta!*" he bellowed as he grabbed the iron fireplace tongs in one hand and the poker in the other. "You won't have any more!"

He flung open the door, heedless of the blast of frigid air, and strode out. "No more, you bastard! Put her the fuck down!"

The wendigo lifted Tara to his mouth again and bit off her head. It rolled along the planks to Diego's feet where it stopped, Tara's sightless eyes staring up at him.

"*Cabron!*" he screamed. He swung for the monster's head as it leaped at him. The iron connected with a ringing blow that numbed Diego's arm. He lifted his right arm to stab at the thing's heart at the same moment it seized his shoulder.

This time he heard the wendigo shriek in agony before the world exploded into a thousand falling shards.

* * * *

"My love, it's good to see you, but a bit shocking all the same." Finn's disembodied voice reached him from somewhere in the strange twilight.

"I don't see anything. Where are we?"

"You've wandered into my Dreaming. Please tell me you are sleeping inside the house."

"I—I think I've had a seizure. I'm out on the porch."

"Ah, my hero. This you will need to

explain to me, but later, when you are safe. I'm coming. Won't take but a moment."

Finn's voice faded, and Diego found himself alone in the featureless, shrouded landscape. He wondered if he would be stuck there forever, without house or tree or even a blade of grass to break the monotony. Then he looked up and saw the stars.

Chapter 17: Plain as Lightning

Diego woke with the leaden disorientation of post-seizure. Light filtered through the window—

Window. He was inside. How and when had he crawled back into the house? And why was he still alive and not possessed?

When he blinked the clouds from his eyes, he saw someone curled up beside him, tousled blue-black hair hiding most of his face. That explained the how at any rate. He hadn't dreamed the conversation with Finn.

"*Cariño?*" Diego reached out to touch his cheek. "God, you're like ice."

Finn's only answer was a soft whimper.

"*Pobre hada.* I dragged you out of your waterbed too soon, didn't I?" Diego rolled over, abused muscles protesting. It hurt like hell to move, but he had no choice. Finn couldn't lie on the hardwood freezing.

He got up on his hands and knees, hooked an arm under Finn's and dragged him inch by painful inch to the ottoman. With a good deal of grunting, he wrestled Finn's long frame up and cocooned him in blankets.

"Good thing you're so light," Diego muttered. *Kitchen. Tea. Aspirin.*

Even the smallest task took a ridiculous amount of time but eventually Diego returned with chamomile tea. He settled next to Finn, put an arm under his shoulders to lift him, and held the mug to his lips. For a moment, he worried Finn might not be responsive enough, then those soft lips moved and parted and he drank in greedy gulps.

"Slowly, slowly, you'll burn your tongue," Diego chided. "Are you with me?"

"Rrmph."

"Not quite, I guess." He put the mug down and nestled under the blankets with Finn in his arms. Even if he was weak and ill, at least he was back in one piece. Finn turned on his side to curl around him, and Diego felt safe enough to go back to sleep.

* * * *

"You feel a little better?" Diego smoothed the hair off Finn's forehead. He had woken to one black eye blinking at him in confusion.

"Oh, assuredly so. Ready to gird myself in salmon scales and battle the white-capped falls."

"No need to be sarcastic. Even if it's poetic sarcasm."

"Your pardon." Finn stretched and let out a slow breath. "I am bone-weary and aching, but no longer dizzy. My love, what possessed you to abandon the safety of the house?"

"It killed Tara McHenry. That nice park ranger who brought your collar back to me."

Diego shuddered and rested his head on Finn's chest. "It was eating her body."

Finn's forehead crinkled. "So you rushed out to rescue someone who was already dead?"

"Yes. I mean, no, I knew I couldn't save her. But I couldn't just stand there and watch her be ripped to shreds."

"But it was no longer her. She was gone. It was simply meat."

Diego squeezed his eyes shut and counted to five. He lacked the energy to explain desecration of the dead. "Finn, if I were dead, would you eat me?"

"Eat—" Finn wrinkled his nose. "Ugh. No. Humans taste disgusting."

"Never mind. The point is that it was taunting me with Tara's body. It threatened more murders, though, that was what got to me." He told Finn everything that had happened and every thought the creature had sent to him.

"A moment. I find myself confused. You

heard it so clearly? You understood it so completely?" Finn tried to sit up and gave up on a little moan.

"Yes, there's no question what it wanted."

"How curious. Its thoughts seemed so indistinct to me, so muddy and jumbled."

"Maybe it's used to talking to humans. Or maybe it was so muddled when it had you the first time because it just woke up."

"Perhaps." Finn chewed on his bottom lip. "And it called you Shaman?"

"Yes. Is that important?"

"It may well be. I must think on it after I have a nap."

Diego stroked a finger over his cheek, his voice cracking as he spoke. "*Mi vida*, we can't think any more. We're out of time. That thing killed because of me and it's going to kill someone else tonight unless I give it what it wants." He closed his eyes against the sting of tears. "You have to keep your promise tonight."

He buried his face against Finn's shoulder, sobs wracking his body.

"Wsht, now." Finn held him close. "While I encouraged you to weep, you need not weep over this. Not yet. The beast is wounded and sleeping. It will not hunt tonight. We have at least that much time, my hero."

"How can you be sure?" Diego choked out.

"I may not understand its thoughts as thoroughly as you, but I hear it quite well. It will not stir tonight." Finn shifted on a little grunt. "Neither will I."

"All right." Diego heaved a shuddering breath. *I don't want this, to be a martyr. I'm just a second-rate writer, not a hero. I just want to run away, to be with him. God, it's not fair.*

"Childish, stupid…" He seized Finn in a fierce hug. They had an extra day and a night, at least, time that needed to be well-spent.

He heaved Finn up on his shoulders, the long body lighter than a human his size, and carried him up to the bed. The rest of the morning, he spoiled Finn without shame with cream, scrambled eggs, roasted chicken, and a long backrub.

"If you were any other man, I would question the motive behind all this kindness." Finn's muffled voice rose from the pillow. "Lie down with me, my love. Let me bask in your heart-fire a bit."

He stripped down to his briefs and slid next to Finn, his skin still cool but no longer icy. The last time he had felt so comfortable simply holding a lover, without anxious thoughts about expectations and who should do what, had been—never. He lay content in Finn's arms, letting his fingers caress over his smooth skin, exploring every dip, valley, and dimple.

Finn's eyes slid shut, his restless body stilled. Diego was so certain he had fallen asleep, the sudden, deep laugh made him jerk back.

"What, *querido*? What's so funny?"

"Oh, m'boy, we are a right pair of fools." Finn still laughed as he rolled onto his back.

"Are we?"

"Sweet mother of us all, yes, we are. Plain as the lightning in your head."

Diego sighed. "If you don't tell me soon, I'm getting up and leaving you here all alone." He gasped when Finn seized his wrist.

"Please don't leave me. I promise to reveal my thoughts. Please don't…"

Diego slid an arm over him and held him tight. "Hey, hey, I wasn't serious. And I wouldn't have gone any farther than the kitchen anyway. What's got into you?"

"Forgive me, my love." Finn shuddered. "A small temporal dislocation. Forgive me."

"You're forgiven. Stop stalling."

"Stalling?"

"It's like ducking the question."

"Ah." Finn gave him a soft kiss. "My hero, you and I both tried to destroy the thing separately. I failed, miserably, because for all my power and experience, I lack the weaponry to harm it. While you harmed it, but still failed to destroy it because you lack control. We need to sally forth together, as one force."

"That's a nice, romantic notion," Diego said with a shake of his head. "But the only time I've hurt it is when I'm flat on my back passed out in a fit. I can't see me being much use in a fight."

"But you see, you've already shown your ability to leave your ailing body behind, to carry on without it when the need is great. Without any apprenticeship, without any knowledge of magic beyond what I have told you, you came to find me when you needed me in a place where you should not have been able to."

Diego sat up, heart thudding. *I'm not*

sure I like where this is going. "But that was an accident. I mean, I didn't know what I was doing."

"Even so, my love. You acted on instinct alone, a sure sign of the incredible, raw power you carry. The beast called you Shaman." Finn stroked a fingertip along his ear, sending a shiver down Diego's back. "It had good reason. Diego, you shine, gods, you could blind a person sometimes. You have more magic in your little finger than some of the fae have in the whole of their long lives."

"But... I thought you said magic flowed through everything. That it's in every pore and strand."

"Yes. True. But in some places and in some beings, the magic concentrates. Think of it as a stream. There is water covering the whole of the streambed but in some places, it merely meanders or trickles, while in others there are dips and rocks and drops. Here the water gains power, the stream rushes and dances, singing with joy."

"I see. I think." Diego's forehead crinkled. "Like you said, though, I don't have any experience, no training, no control. How does knowing I have something I can't use help us?"

Finn spread a palm over his chest. "I could supply the control. If you are willing. Guide you and show you what you must do."

"While I'm in the middle of a seizure."

"Yes, my love. I have heard you, have felt the tendrils of your thoughts reach out to me. It can be done. Of course, you open your channels most during lovemaking."

"Oh. Look, if you wanted sex, you could just ask for it instead of all th—"

Finn gripped his arms hard, a red tinge in his eyes. "No. This is not some convoluted ploy to gain a few moments' mating with you. I will not lose you, Diego. Listen to me."

"Sorry. I'm listening."

"We must have you in the midst of a fit because we must have your lightning. I must be able to reach you easily to keep you with me. You are so closely walled most of the time; it would take far too much effort to break through. If you open to me of your own accord, it will be swifter and more pleasant for you as well."

"Please don't dig your claws into my arms," Diego murmured, as his thoughts skittered around in circles. It was a chance Finn offered, one he thought they did not have, one that offered life and love at the end rather than darkness.

He tried for something close to a smile. "So you're saying you want to practice, is that it?"

"Yes. We must be certain you are ready before the thing wakes again."

Diego ran a finger down Finn's long nose. "I'm scared to death, OK? But I trust you and I'm willing, even though I'll feel like crud afterward. It's kind of hard to get in the mood when you're so serious, though."

"Oh, my love, you might as well slay me now." Finn flung his arms wide in a dramatic gesture. "I have been called many unflattering things but never serious."

"That's better," Diego whispered as he leaned in to slide his lips over Finn's. The soft touch sparked. Finn lifted his head to meet him and the kiss caught and blossomed to roaring flame. Finn's long fingers stroked over his back and arms, petal soft, sending shivers over his skin.

"Would you like to take me, my hero?" Finn murmured against his jaw. "I may be a bit lacking in stamina at the moment."

Diego moaned as a sweet ache rushed up from his groin. He slid between Finn's legs with his lips fastened tight on that long, pale throat. Finn's hands slid onto his butt over the cotton, then under the waistband to knead his cheeks. The sensual slide of elastic down his backside made him squirm, rubbing their hardening cocks together in delicious ways.

He lifted his head to look in Finn's eyes. "Do you like it? Having someone hammering into you?" Some of his lovers over the years would have rather died than take bottom.

"Yes." Finn bent his knees up. "Oh, most assuredly yes."

Diego took his face between his hands and kissed him softly. "I love you so," he whispered before he captured Finn's lips in a searing kiss. His hips ground against him in time to their heartbeats while Finn's hands wandered his body in soft caresses.

"Jar. By your head." He motioned for the petroleum jelly on the nightstand. When Finn handed it to him, he pushed back on his knees to uncap the jar and dip his fingers in. He curled forward to kiss the tip of Finn's erection, lying hard and ready on his stomach. The spice of his musk filled his head, wild and erotic and somehow so clean, wild mint and honey, river and basil.

He closed his fingers around Finn's shaft, stroking softly while his lubed fingers slid between Finn's cheeks.

"Diego..." Finn arched into his attentions and spread his knees wider. "I don't need as much time beforehand as you. I want you so."

"Dangerously close to 'take me now', *mi vida*," Diego said on a soft chuckle. He slipped the pad of his forefinger in all the same, unwilling to take Finn unprepared. The groan torn from Finn's chest was passion soaked and achingly sweet.

With a last, heated kiss to the slick head of Finn's member, he positioned himself with one hand and teased at the tight ring. He met only a moment's resistance before he slipped inside.

"God… oh… Finn…" he gasped out. The sheath gripped him so tight, the channel so smooth and cool, like nothing he had ever felt before. All thoughts of why they were making love skittered away, chased off by the rising tide of pleasure.

He sank within slowly, hands on either side of Finn, and then those long arms closed around him to pull him down. An odd, dizzy feeling of surrender washed over him. *On top, yes, but not in control. And it's so damn good this way.*

Finn moved beneath him, gentle rolls of his hips, encouraging his thrusts, setting the rhythm. His body tightened with need within a few, short minutes. "Finn… Finn…"

"That's it. I love you, Diego. More than sun and rain. Ride me as if you rode the storm wind," Finn murmured against his ear.

Diego gasped and thrust faster, plunging

deep with each hard stroke. "Yes… *dios…* oh, yes…" His body compressed to a single need, a single, overwhelming, mounting pressure. Three short cries leapt from him as he hung on that almost-there moment of agonized pleasure. With a long groan, he buried his face against Finn's shoulder and came in a rushing plunge, hips bucking hard through each forceful spasm.

Blue fire danced over Finn's skin and shone through the hand he lifted to cup Diego's face. *Forgive me, my love.* The whispered thought caressed his mind.

Finn's body seemed consumed by the blue flames in the last instant before Diego's vision burst into a hundred thousand exploding stars.

* * * *

With a terrier-tenacious grip, Finn kept Diego with him as he slipped into the Dreaming.

He had told Diego it was not a place. In a physical sense, this was true. A state of consciousness, yes, it was that, but his love had managed to knock on the door of his mind and wander in—well he had never been much of a philosopher. Things were or they were not. One did better to adapt when a new thing occurred.

Chapter 18: Practice

The mind Finn embraced had touched his in more than one lifetime. The physical manifestation had been different the last time, the body larger, the personality more confident and carefree, but still the same shining soul. Even in his most awakened lifetime, though, Diego had not summoned lightning.

"My hero? Are you well?"

The mental image of Diego shook his head. "It's so... strange. I feel like I'm really sitting here with you."

"You are. In a way. Your thoughts nestled next to mine. I thought this would be a better way for you to begin. Rather than seeing your own body from outside."

Diego shuddered. "Right. I might've thought I was dead." He stared upward for a long moment. "Finn? What are all the stars? What do they mean?"

"They are merely stars."

"You're such a liar."

"Yes."

"I'd rather you told me it's none of my business than have you fib to me."

"Fib?"

"A small lie. One that doesn't necessarily hurt anyone."

Finn chuckled. "Ah, they come in degrees and types now. I like that."

Even connected like this, Diego kept much of his mind closed off. Finn waited while he mulled something over behind his walls.

"Why doesn't it hurt you when I seize?" he finally asked.

"I feel your lightning, love, it sparks and hisses. But you do not hurl it at me."

"But why?"

"You know when you are in danger and when you are safe," Finn answered as simply as he could. "While you have not been aware that you acted to save yourself, your instincts have held."

Again the shuttered, solitary thinking. *This would be much easier, m'boy, if you simply let the battlements down.*

"I heard that. I can't help if my thoughts aren't all out in the open. *Cariño*, if I'm seizing now, why can't I see the lightning?"

"State of mind, my hero. Everything here is thought, not the sight you have with your eyes."

"Wait. All I have to do is think about the lightning?"

"Something like, yes."

A thunder-roll of irritation rippled from Diego. "I thought you said you would help me figure it out."

"Perhaps it is like when we sat at the table and you tried to explain art to me. I could not find anything to hold onto in the explanation until I had seen it for myself."

"Nice analogy. Not helping."

Finn pointed up. "You asked about the stars. Reach for one. Take it down."

"What? I can't—"

"You must put aside your stubborn disbelief, my love. It's become rather tiresome."

"Fine, fine," Diego grumbled, and reached up. At first, he snatched at emptiness and Finn despaired that he would be unable to let go of himself enough. As he stared at the stars, though, he became entranced and his light grew from golden to white-hot. He reached up and closed his thoughts around—

"Diego, no! Not that one!"

Too late.

* * * *

"Moira, tell them! You know him! He's not evil!" The man's features contorted in anguish and frustration, his flame-red hair sparking in the last fingers of sunset.

"But he is. He took you from me and he's bewitched you. For you I do this," she answered, cold and flat. She refused to look at him.

Agony, unbearable agony—the iron spike through his chest, the iron shackling him to the cage, cold, so cold, the pain so sharp it robbed him of speech and breath...

* * * *

"Holy shit! What the hell was that?"

"A memory, my love," Finn answered softly. "One I didn't wish for you to see."

"God. Warn a person next time." Diego's light shivered and wavered from the shock. He faded behind his walls again, thinking. "That's what happened, wasn't it? What drove you into the Dreaming for so many centuries. You loved him, she loved him, she was jealous so she went to the authorities screaming witchcraft."

"Yes. But I loved her as well. It was a terrible thing she did. One I still can't fathom. They... caged him. Tortured him. They burned him when he would not confess to things he had not done. As his 'demon familiar' I was made to watch. Too weak to protect him, too wounded to save him, I could not stop them. Then they dismembered me and tossed me in the river."

"*Cariño*, I'm so sorry. I didn't mean—"

"Hush, my love. Done is done. Of course your mind would be drawn to the memories you share with me."

Diego faded to gray, and for a moment, Finn thought he might be shocked back to the waking world. He whispered, "The man with the red hair... was me?"

"Yes, love. Yes. We had a short few months together that time."

"Finn—"

"Wsht. Console me later. We have work

to do." Finn pointed again, this time to a specific spot. "Try there. You may find that one to be more helpful. And less upsetting."

With a quicksilver shimmer, Diego recovered enough to reach out again.

* * * *

The man's fingers caressed his harp strings. It was as if he called the wind into his music, the rustle of the leaves and rush of water.

He watched and listened from the shadows he had pulled about him. Not fearful, merely cautious. Humans could be so strange. But this one's heart shone so bright, his blood sang so clear and true, how could he be anything but a friend? He took on a songbird shape and hopped into the sunlight.

"Good morning, little one." The man smiled. "Did you come to join me in my song?" He cocked his head to one side, white-blond hair gleaming in the light. "Though you are no more bird than I am fish. I hope you do not hide yourself out of fear of me."

The man put his harp down and his smile grew brighter. "Here. I will show you what I learned today." When he stretched out his hand, a tiny whirlwind grew on his palm. The nest of wind tugged at the air and became a miniature cloud. The cloud hovered over his hand, gray as a dove's wings and plump with moisture. Upon his skin, mist-sized raindrops fell.

A laugh like a stream in spring flood leaped from him…

*　*　*　*

"There, my love, was that one better?"

Diego hugged him tight. "I felt it! I felt what he did! Reaching, yes, a kind of twist of thought. But it's more than that. I could feel him… it… connect!" In his excitement, he tore himself from Finn's grasp and vanished from the Dreaming.

Finn opened his eyes to find Diego's essence staring at his body convulsing on the bed.

That's disturbing...

"I feared it would be." Finn sat up with a sigh. "You must not lose contact with me when we face the beast. Please."

Sorry. I got so caught up. The man with the harp, that was me, too, wasn't it?

"Indeed. A different you, but you all the same. From long, long ago."

Was that... Diego's shimmer flickered and rippled. *Was that the first time we met?*

"Yes, my hero. The very first. I loved you from that first moment. Sometimes it takes me longer to recognize you than others. Most times, you have no memory of me at all. But it is always good to find you again."

Did you know me on the bridge? Is that

why you came with me?

"Not in that moment, no. I was frightened and in pain and simply saw a bright, shining heart, without guile or malice. And then I did not wish to see, hid the knowledge from myself to guard my own heart."

You're not going to tell me. When you knew.

"If you must know, it was when you brought me the crayons," Finn grumbled. "Enough. Concentrate. Do you see your lightning now?"

Yes, I think so. Like fireflies.

Finn wrapped his arms around Diego's shimmer to guide him since Diego still thought of himself as a physical being. "Gather it together. On your palm if you like, as you saw with the little cloud. Feel how it sings to you, through you, for it is yours. Yours to command. That's it, m'boy, sing with it, ask of it, try to—"

The ball of lightning suddenly grew to

the size of Diego's head. He whirled and flung it out the open window. A sharp crack split the air and fire blossomed in the sky, bright enough to rival the afternoon sun.

Like that?

Finn stared at him in shock, unable to recall how words were formed. He cleared his throat twice, his voice shaking when he spoke. "Yes, love, something like. Just like. That was... how did you do that?"

It sort of... told me how. It just felt right.

"Do that tomorrow night and I don't think we need worry," he said on a grim chuckle. "But pray be certain you don't hit me instead."

I'll do my best, mi vida. *How do I get back into my body?*

"Ah, for that he still needs me." Finn swept him a little bow and held out his hand as if asking for a dance. "With your permission?"

Diego's hand of white light settled in his

and Finn led his essence back to his body, lifted it and settled it back where it belonged. The twitching, flailing body immediately quieted and Diego was once more ensconced behind his walls.

He tried to recall all the things Diego would need when he woke and fetched extra blankets, the little bottle of white pills and water. His heart still hammered, but he slid under the covers to take Diego in his arms and send warmth to his chilled body.

Chapter 19: Heart of Ice

"Finn?"

"Hmm?"

"Could you stop a minute? I need to show you something." Diego waited while Finn drew a few more curls on a Gordian knot of Caribbean Green and Cornflower.

He had hoped they would be able to surprise the wendigo while it slept that morning, but Finn said it would be impossible. With a spirit of wind and ice, he insisted, one had to wait until it manifested and that would not be until evening.

"I've set the phone up on speed dial. In case something happens or if you need help and I... can't help you anymore, I want you to be able to call Tia Carmen." He held the phone out so Finn could see the numbers. "Press any one of these top buttons and you'll be able to talk to her, all right?"

"And if she is not at home when it shrieks?"

"Rings, *mi vida*, we say a phone rings. Then you'll hear a click and Tia Carmen's voice will tell you she isn't home. The answering machine. You know how that works. When it beeps, you say you called, turn the phone off, and stay close until she calls you back. Do you have all that?"

Finn's forehead crinkled. "It seems simple enough."

"You don't sound sure."

"I will do what I must when I must, never fear," Finn said, with a dismissive wave. Then he scrubbed his hands over his face with a sigh. "My love, if you did not need rest, I would ask you to walk with me in the woods. I feel a melancholy humor creeping into my blood which we can ill afford today."

"I know. Me, too." Diego chewed on his bottom lip. "Let's take our lunch out onto the porch. Almost like being in the woods, right?"

Only a small dark stain on the wood near the window remained of the horrible scene two nights before. The wendigo had taken Tara's head and body when it fled, and Finn had whisked the remaining blood and gore away on a stream of water he coaxed from the air.

The dark patch was reminder enough, though. Diego shivered despite the warm sun on his back. Finn pulled him onto the porch swing and held him tight while he sang to him in the soft, earth-and-water tones of ancient Gaelic.

They stayed wrapped in each other's arms until the sun settled atop the pines.

Diego broke the silence. "We should get ready."

"Would you like the bed again, then?"

"No, *cariño*. I think it's best if I stay out here. If things reach the point where you need to let it possess me, both you and it have to be able to get to me easily."

"I won't let—"

"Sh, hush." Diego put a finger over his lips. "I know. You want to protect me this time because the last time you couldn't. But unless you've been spinning some pretty incredible lies, all you have to do is wait until I come back again in another body, right? Somehow, I get the feeling there's not the same option if you die."

"I couldn't say," Finn answered on a hard swallow. "I've never died before."

"Right. The price of immortality. But if everything I've ever heard or read is right, if one of the fae is destroyed, that's it, you're toast."

Finn's brows drew together. "I don't think I would become a slice of heated bread…"

"Sorry, stupid expression. I mean, I don't think you get to come back again."

"So I have been given to understand as well."

Diego took his face between his hands.

"You need to keep your promise. Back off if the time comes. Let it happen. End it quickly. Don't let me linger."

"But—"

"No. No wheedling, no arguments. You need to swear to me you'll do what I need you to do."

"I—" Finn heaved a shaky breath. "I do so swear, by the waters that sustain me. I will not permit you to linger in horror and anguish."

"Thank you." Diego leaned in to give him a swift, hard hug. "Ready?"

"I've certainly had more romantic propositions," Finn grumbled. "Give me a kiss and tell me you love me and I shall be."

Diego conjured a smile and leaned in to brush his lips against Finn's. "I love you," he breathed against his jaw.

"Mmm, much better," Finn murmured, and seized his mouth in a hard kiss, almost bruising in its desperate passion. He rose, slid out of his jeans and spread a blanket out in front of the porch swing. "Lie down, my love. No, leave your clothes on, if you would."

"Um, why?"

"I fear your body will chill as it is. Best keep something on."

"Good point." *But I love the feel of your hands on my skin.* "I'm not sure I can do this."

Finn knelt and crawled up between his thighs. He eased the waistband of Diego's track pants down and snugged the elastic up under his balls. "You have said that before. I didn't believe you then either."

"But my stomach's all in knots and I don't—oh, my God." Diego's hips jerked up as Finn bent down to wrap his incredible tongue all the way around the head of his cock. The rush of blood to his groin left him dizzy and panting.

"I begin to think it must be some necessary ritual for you, to protest that you cannot. I shan't take it to heart," Finn murmured against his skin. He returned his mouth to Diego, lips and tongue wrapped around his shaft in a double embrace.

"Oh... Finn..." Diego buried his fingers in the cool silk of his hair, black water through his fingers. "That feels so damn good."

Mi vida, I want to do this for years to come. I want you with me always. I don't want this to end...

He rolled his hips to match the rhythm Finn set. The breeze carried the spice of their mingled arousal to him and his heart sped. Lips fastened hard around his erection, Finn increased his speed. Anxious fear leaped through him, but the adrenaline rush only added to the arousal.

Strange, I shouldn't be... oh, Finn...

I hear you, love. Finn's thoughts came to him, clear and warm. *Hold tight, stay close.*

The tightening rush of orgasm hit half a breath before the seizure. The sudden lurch and plunge terrified him. For a moment, he fell into an endless abyss but soon blue light enveloped him, cradling him in a tender love song…

Finn?

"Oof, bucko, you do enjoy frightening the mischief out of me, don't you?" Finn finished covering the convulsing body on the porch and rose.

What do you mean? He regarded his body, disoriented, unable to recognize himself.

"How you jerked away. I had a wee bit of trouble catching you up."

Sorry. Do you need a minute?

Finn's fingers closed on the air in the now-familiar gesture of negation. "Do you? You seem a bit wavery, my hero."

He tore his attention away from his face, slack-jawed and drooling. *How can anyone stand to look at me again after watching that?*

"The fits are distressing," Finn answered softly. "But more because you suffer than because of the contortions you are forced through."

Very sweet, but still—

"You must shed your self-doubt now, Diego." Finn's shape melted as he advanced, his human form stretching and expanding. The nightmare steed from his first encounter with the wendigo stood before him, tossing his head. "Your warrior spirit has lain dormant, but it must live in you still. Mount, my hero. Hunt with me."

A shudder of dislocation ran through Diego. The wendigo had demanded the same thing. *Dammit, Finn, how am I supposed to mount without a body? I don't even know how to ride.*

Horse-Finn stamped a hoof. "You are without the limits of flesh now. And you must maintain the connection yourself. I will have other things to devour my attention. For the love of all the gods, stop dallying. The beast begins to stir, and we will soon lose the sun."

While his limbs appeared made of translucent, golden light, Diego still felt as if he had a body. Probably part of the problem. He struggled to recall how it had felt the day before, reaching for Finn's stars, pulling in the lightning. Then, as if he stepped sideways though a half-open door, he found that strange angle of consciousness again. Finn's blue glow beckoned to him, not the horse, not the man-shape, but the true core of his being.

So beautiful... The connection between them materialized for him, bright tendrils, rainbow hued, bridges between their bodies and their essences, stretching back through the centuries.

He came to Finn and nestled close against him, closer than two bodies could ever be. Finn's anxiety hit him with such poignancy he wanted to weep, but the love enveloping him, heated and deep-rooted, gave him strength. He envisioned himself mounted on Finn's back and found his view of the world elevated to a greater height than he was used to.

"Much better, love. Stay with me." Finn snorted and took off at a breakneck gallop.

It's awake?

"Stirring. Considering. It feels you coming." Finn jumped a fallen pine without breaking stride. "I think it's curious."

So we're in time? It hasn't killed again?

"Not yet. It's famished. Don't you feel it?"

I don't... As if the thought had conjured it, the wendigo's chill chasm of hunger reached out for him. *God... Finn... it feels like it wants to swallow the world whole.*

"If it could find a way, it most likely would." Finn took a sharp turn and thundered uphill, out of the trees, hooves striking sparks on the rocky ground. "It comes, my hero. You must be ready, but you do not stand alone."

I know, mi vida. *Neither do you.* Despite the distance from his body, he still found his lightning when he reached for it. Power flooded through him, dangerous, intoxicating.

Underneath him Finn surged forward, muscles bunching and flexing as his body took on yet more mass, sleek, black scales growing up to cover horsehair. The beat of huge wings replaced the drum of hooves. Challenge roared from Dragon-Finn's throat.

The wendigo's answering howl echoed off the hillsides.

Shaman. Its colder than the void thought knifed into his. *Banish your spirit guide and come to me. Send it away or I will take another.*

I won't let—

With hurricane force, the wendigo manifested in an icy blast, both physical and psychic. Its size and shape remained elusive, though a shimmer on the wind showed where it passed. Finn struggled to keep aloft, cursing as he flung up a barrier to shield Diego.

No, querido, don't let it distract you. Diego nudged the barrier back down. *Concentrate on attack. I won't lose you.*

"Best not, bucko," Finn growled. "And take your own advice."

A two-story wall of water rose from the nearby stream and slammed into the wendigo's shimmer. It only wavered for a moment before it renewed its onslaught.

Your spirit guide is nothing, shaman. Powerless. Come to me. Feel true power.

The fierce winds tumbled Finn from the sky. He landed awkwardly on the rocks, one wing pinned beneath him. "Blasted, cursed, evil bag of wind," he muttered as he struggled to rise. "Diego, do you have it? I could use some help. Just a mite."

Almost, almost... are you all right? He tried his best to concentrate on gathering the lightning, but Finn's pain was terrible. The wing or the leg or both had most likely snapped.

"Destroy that wretched thing and I will be."

The ball of lightning gathered on his palm and grew from an orange lick of flame to blue to a white-hot maelstrom of crackling plasma. He felt as much as saw the wendigo bearing down on Finn, and he hurled his lightning into the center of the tempest. The winds shrieked, the monster's progress halted.

Then to Diego's horror, it turned and fled, not into the wilderness but toward town.

"Never fear, my hero. It shan't get far." Finn rid himself of the broken wing and reformed as a Rottweiler-sized black falcon. He arrowed through the gathering dusk, gaining swiftly on the wendigo, whose passage wavered and meandered as if it were dizzy.

The lights of a house shone through the trees. A small child played in the patch of grass by the back door.

No! Finn, get in front of it!

With a tremendous burst of speed, Finn swooped in to cut the wendigo off from the house. It shrieked its frustration and took physical form, perhaps hoping to reach the child on the ground. On all fours, it loped toward the toddler, who sat frozen and helpless in horror.

Don't panic, don't panic... Grim determination overrode terror. Diego pulled the lightning to him in a vertiginous rush, only half-aware, he formed a spear instead of a ball. *Wendigo! Leave the child alone!*

The cadaverous, mottled face lifted to him, mouth stretched in a manic leer. He hurled his spear directly at its heart. The lightning struck true, the spear shattered against its heart of ice, and the wendigo turned to stagger back into the trees.

Now the toddler recalled how to move and dashed into the house, screaming, "Mommy, Mommy, there's a monster outside and an angel fighting him!"

Diego heard the mother reply in a distracted fashion as she closed the door, "That's nice, hon."

Once again Finn shifted, this time to a black bear to match the speed of the wendigo through the forest. "Damn you, coward! Turn and fight!" he roared, as they crashed through a bramble-heavy thicket.

The wendigo stumbled on, wounded, unable to return to its most powerful, incorporeal form. Its thoughts had gone silent though, so Diego did not discount the possibility of a ruse to draw Finn into a trap. The thicket became so thick they could no longer see their quarry, though the snapping, rustling sounds asserted he still ran ahead.

Watch yourself, mi vida, it's not done yet.

"I know that, love. Don't you think I—"

The sudden crash of brush on Finn's

right cut him off. A heavy body hit his side and slammed him to the ground. He cried out as claws like scythes raked deep into his flesh. Sharp teeth flashed. Bear-Finn got hold of the wendigo's throat. In a hideous show of strength, the wendigo took hold of Finn's jaws and pulled them apart, until the bottom one broke with a sickening snap. It lifted Finn over its head and hurled him against an ancient pine. He landed in an unnaturally twisted heap, his back broken.

Finn! Dios... Finn!

I'm still here, my hero. Please forgive me. I can't—

Sh, sh, I'll finish it. I have to. Finn... I love you.

Diego? What are you going to do?

With a soft caress over Finn's mind, Diego shut himself off from his love, though his heart broke to hear Finn's anguish. He turned to the wendigo, which stood, waiting, as if it knew this moment had always been inevitable.

I have defeated your spirit guide three times, shaman. You are too powerful to depend on such a weak being. It is time. Join with me.

Diego had no intention of giving in yet. His lightning had hurt the monster, but not destroyed it. He needed a larger missile, a more massive gathering of magic than he had attempted before. He pulled the lightning to him once more, gathering a ball as large as a mine shell. *Not enough, it's not enough.*

In desperation, he cast out farther, reaching for something more to help him, and was shocked to find tendrils of magic connecting him to the trees, the rocks, the tiny lichen at his feet. Not bridges or paths, but an incredible shining web of connections. Exhilarated and frightened by so much power, he opened himself to the flows, let the energy flood through him.

Shaman, you cannot destroy me this way. Wound me, banish me for a time, but I will live on.

He ignored the wendigo's taunts and kept at it. The ball expanded to the size of a small tank. When he prepared to hurl it, though, he had another hard shock.

The web connected him to the wendigo. This horrific, destructive creature was part of the magic as well, part of the fabric, the whole. The cold void inside it howled with ravenous hunger and desperate longing, but its connections to the world around it shone no less brightly than Diego's.

He lowered his arms and let the lightning scatter.

You see now. We must be one, Shaman. The wendigo opened its arms in a dreadful parody of a lover's welcome. *Come to me.*

The void must be filled, Tia Carmen had said. The terrible hunger had to be satisfied. It occurred to him suddenly that the stories of pouring hot wax down a wendigo's throat were a metaphor for something else.

Diego moved into the wendigo's embrace. Nature abhors a vacuum. *Finn, help me do what I need to do.*

My love, you can't expect me to help you be possessed. Finn's thoughts came to him full of bleak despair.

No. Help me. Lend me your strength, your fire.

I don't under—oh. My hero, this is perilous.

So help me, dammit.

The wendigo's touch flung him into an empty blackness. Gripping cold stole his thoughts; the yawning chasm of need ripped a scream of despair from him. Finn came to him, stood shoulder to shoulder with him against the dark.

The things I do for you, my hero.

Diego didn't answer. He used Finn's love as an anchor, a starting point, and began to weave a different sort of lightning, a liquid stream of magic into which he poured his own warmth, his kindness, his love of the world.

Rather than hurl this magic, he poured it into the void, on and on, though it seemed only a drop in an ocean of frigid emptiness. He wavered, uncertain and afraid.

Go on, my love. I think you have it right. Finn's essence embraced his, shoring him up, lending him courage. A bright pinprick appeared in the void, the first sign of thaw in an endless winter.

The wendigo shrieked and flung up a wall of howling ice to block the fledgling light, a shield behind which to mount its own attack. Bolt after bolt of black despair slammed into Diego. *Failure*, the wind shrieked at him. *At everything you set your hand to. A fraud, a sham. Your every effort comes to nothing. You bring only pain to those who love you.*

He faltered and dropped some of the

threads he wove. His father's voice thundered in his memory, *I won't believe my son is a... a faggot! It's a stage, an illness...* The voice of his college advisor joined him. *It's not as if everyone can be Hemingway, Diego. We have dozens of students come through here each year who write better than you...* Mitch's sneer came back to him. *Like you're fucking Jack Kerouac or something. Well, you're not. And you never will be...*

Don't listen to them, beloved! Finn shouted down the memories. *It rakes your thoughts for your darkest moments! Don't listen! You are brave and strong and... and a bard worthy of the High King's table!*

A laugh bubbled up despite the barrage of despair. The laugh shoved the darkness back a hair, and for a moment, he caught a glimpse of himself through Finn's eyes, a shining being of white light, shot through with threads of golden magic. He spread his arms and reached out once more, stretching farther into the bright web.

The trees, the birds, the streams, the very ground beneath their feet all contributed to the outpouring of heat. The bridges of connections multiplied into infinite webs, every cricket, every blade of grass, every life lending its light, its strength, its notes. The weaving became a song so bright and complex, Diego's heart threatened to burst with joy.

With a piercing howl, the wendigo attacked, claws and teeth of ice sinking into him, trying to rip him away from Finn and from the tendrils of magic. Diego grappled with it, discordant notes knifing into the magic as they raged back and forth, heat of the sun battling the howling chill of the void.

The liquid stream of song had taken root in the core of the wendigo's being and would not be dislodged. Note by note, the void filled, the light growing in the vast chasm of despair. Diego clung fast as he felt the monster weaken.

In desperation, it tried to attack Finn and hurled a bolt of black rage at his essence. Finn answered by throwing up a wall of blue fire to block the missile and adding his own voice to the song.

The wendigo shrieked, clawing at the magic invading its being, tearing itself to pieces as the emptiness filled. The chill dissipated, the light of the world melted its heart of ice. There was peace where there had been emptiness, calm where there had been raging despair.

The howling wind died down as the wendigo's essence scattered. Diego found himself back in the woods by the tree where Finn lay. The malevolent spirit no longer inhabited the world. Only its magic remained to join the song, a whisper on the wind.

Cariño, *will you be all right?*

"Won't be but a moment, my hero. I need a shape that doesn't require a backbone," Finn said as his bear shape contracted into a large bumblebee.

All right. I'm just so tired now.

Finn snorted, an odd sound from a bumblebee. "I would think so, m'dear. You only worked more magic in a night than I've seen any other man work in a lifetime."

Chapter 20: Waiting

Finn stared morosely at Diego's body, so terribly still and pale as death. Back behind the walls of his mind, Finn could not reach him, and he had retreated so deeply, he could no longer hear him either.

"I don't think this is good, my love," he murmured. "You just don't look well at all."

The prolonged seizure and a night in the chill while Finn tried to put himself back together properly could not have done any good. He had carried Diego inside as soon as he could and wrapped him in blankets, but he still would not wake.

As much as it pained him to admit, Diego needed human help. He picked up the phone and tried to recall everything Diego had said.

"Buttons… buttons… the ones at the top," he muttered. He pressed one and then another. Nothing happened. Near panic, he shook the phone and was about to fling it across the room when he recalled a little red light came on when someone's voice came through. The large, blue button in the center, yes, that's how Diego said one 'turned it off'. Perhaps it worked the other way as well.

He pressed and received a contented sort of hum from the thing. *Good. It's happy with me.* Then he tried the top button on the left again. The hum stopped, replaced by little tones and then a shrill sound. *Ringing*, that was the word.

"*Hola?*"

Oh, thank the gods... "I need help, dear lady, please. Or Diego does. I'm at a loss."

"Finn?"

"Yes, yes, it's me. He had an over-long seizure, he won't wake, how do I get help for him?"

"Why did he have such a terrible one?"

Another time he would have loved to tell the story in loving and graphic detail, but his worry kept him to short, terse sentences.

"Don't worry, *querido*. I'll call Ms Thorpe. She'll get help to the house. You stay by him. Keep him warm. There will be men coming in a truck with flashing lights. The truck might make a loud, screaming sound. You must not be afraid of these things. They'll help Diego."

"I will do my best."

"Keep the phone with you. I'll call again in a little while."

"Yes, ma'am."

He waited for what seemed an interminable amount of time before the men in the screaming, flashing truck finally arrived. They took in what he told them and worked quickly to bundle Diego onto a little cot with wheels.

"You will be gentle with him?" he asked,

his heart already aching to think of Diego being taken from him.

One of the men gave him an odd look. "You related? We could let you come with."

"No, I'm his lover."

The second man shook his head while the first shot him a quelling glance. "Sorry, then. You understand, eh? I mean, you can always follow in your car if you want or call the hospital to see how he's doing."

"Yes. Thank you. I'll stay here."

The men put Diego in the back of the truck and drove off. Finn sat on the front porch with the phone in both hands and though he tried to be brave, he couldn't quite keep the tears from his voice when Tia Carmen called again. She told him the name of the place where Diego had been taken and reassured him that he would get the care he needed.

"Tia Carmen? Will you... is there some way to speak to him?"

"When he wakes, *querido*. There will be a phone in his hospital room. But no one knows how long he will sleep."

"He was so brave, so brilliant. You should have seen him."

"I'm glad that the wind spirit's balance has been restored, but I think I would have been too frightened to watch," she said on a little chuckle.

"If you speak to him, could you tell him… tell him I will wait for him here?"

"I'll tell him. He will be glad to hear it."

For the next two weeks, Finn spent an inordinate amount of time on his back, staring up at the sky. The only thing Tia Carmen could tell him was Diego was 'stable', whatever in blazes that meant, and that he still had not woken.

He sank into a swamp of melancholy, unable to extricate himself. It was too ridiculous, of course. For centuries, he had lived alone, mating where he would, keeping his own counsel for the most part. These intrusions of mortal lovers, the way they seized his heart and held it fast, still puzzled him.

When he thought back over the years, though, he realized the one who captured him for more than a single night, again and again, had always been the same. Six times he had found his Taliesin again in another vessel. This was the seventh.

Tia Carmen said Diego had woken briefly, twice. The doctors were baffled, since physically, he appeared well. Of course, they were human doctors and failed to understand the psychic toll exacted in defeating the wendigo.

Inside the house, the phone rang. He leapt up and dashed inside to snatch it up before the smug little answering machine could.

"Thorpe residence."

"Finn, *caro*, it's Carmen. Diego is awake, but very weak still. He has arranged to send you a present, though. A truck should bring the box today. He says the driver will leave it on the porch if you don't show yourself. You are to take out the silver disc first and watch it before you touch anything else in the box, and when you do use them, make sure you do it outside. Do you know how to work the DVD?"

"Deeveedee?"

"The machine that swallows the silver discs and shows them to you on the television."

"Oh. Yes. Diego has shown me. I watch the moving drawings sometimes. *Anime*, he calls them. Charming stories."

"*Bueno*. Are you all right, *querido*? You sound so tired."

"I am well enough, dear lady. Though I hesitate to tell you what I would give to hear his voice. Or better yet, to hold him again."

"Soon, soon." He heard the smile in her voice. "You are impatient for someone who has lived so long."

"Yes. So I have always been told."

The truck with the box arrived that afternoon, driven by a lovely woman with beautiful legs visible below her short, brown pants. Dog-Finn greeted her on the porch, tail thumping against the planks. She rang the bell, waited for a bit, ruffled Finn's ears and left the box as Tia Carmen said would happen.

Finn waited until the truck disappeared through the trees, and then shifted back to his own form to tear it open right there on the porch. *Oh, such fascinating things...* Strange little implements with tufts of hair on the end, bits of wood, and some large rectangles of some sort of cloth mounted on frames greeted him. Best of all, though, was the collection of brightly colored tubes. The arrangement reminded him of his crayons, which could only be a good thing.

"Ah, there you are." He pulled out the silver disc and rushed back into the house to watch what it had to say. Soft music played and some incomprehensible lines and squiggles flashed across the screen. Then a rich-voiced little man with curly hair began to speak about 'the basics of oil painting'.

Finn watched in rapt fascination to learn the secrets Jasper Johns knew.

* * * *

Sheila drove up to the house again to check on things. Someone was staying at the Thorpe place, she was told, but since she'd started her new job at Fundy, she'd never seen a soul. There was a truck parked in the drive, sure, but it never moved an inch, and a big, black dog sometimes lay on the front porch, but no one ever came out when it barked.

The truck was there, as always. The dog was nowhere in sight. She was about to turn around and drive off when she spotted a gorgeous side of beefcake at the side of the house. He sat at an easel, brush in one hand, artist's palette in the other, his incredible, long black hair falling loose down his bare back.

She chuckled at herself, palms sweating, as she grabbed her ranger's hat from the front seat and got out to say hello.

"Morning," she said with a wave as he turned toward her. "Sheila LeBan, Fundy Park Service. Thought I'd stop by, see if everything's all right. Knew someone's staying here. Hadn't seen hide nor hair of you, though."

The man watched her approach with one brow raised before he flashed a beautiful, disarming smile. "I'm Finn. I have been here, though I do go for long walks and such."

"Guess so. Artist needs his inspiration, eh? Watcha painting there?" The blue and white swirls bore no resemblance to anything she could see.

He turned back to his canvas, head

cocked to one side. "Wind."

"Oh, sure, you betcha. I see that." She saw nothing like it, but wanted to keep the chiseled hunk talking. "That what you're up here for? Get some painting done?"

Finn let out a little sigh. "Truthfully, I'm waiting."

She thought he was going to say more, but then he straightened and turned toward the road in an attitude of listening. A red Expedition turned onto the gravel drive and climbed the little hill toward the house. Finn rose, radiating anticipation. He placed his things down on his chair, watching the truck with such intensity, she thought he might burn holes in the tires with his eyes.

A woman rolled out of the driver's seat, older, overweight. That couldn't possibly be what he was waiting for, could it? But no, Finn stayed rooted to the spot. Then the passenger door opened and a man climbed out. The way he moved, Sheila mistook him for old and decrepit. He eased out of the cab, retrieved a cane from inside, and clung to the door while he got his balance. When he raised his head, though, she saw a young, handsome face and a smile that put the sun to shame.

"Diego!" Finn bellowed as he barreled down the hill to sweep him up in his arms. He planted a fierce, demanding kiss on his passenger's lips, going at it like it was the last kiss he'd ever get.

No question about it, not even a hint of doubt. She grinned as she watched Finn sweep Diego round and round in dizzy, happy circles. Love shone there, as clear as the day was long, and despite her moment of disappointment, she couldn't help the warm glow knowing his wait was over.

The woman waddled up the drive to greet her and introduce herself as Miriam Thorpe. "You're new here, aren't you?"

"Yep. Just a couple weeks ago."

They watched as Diego smoothed the hair back from Finn's forehead, talking to him in soft, urgent tones.

"Well, damn," Sheila said on a little laugh. "All the good ones are taken or gay and these two are both. They do make a handsome couple though, eh?"

Miriam snorted. "So long as he keeps Diego happy and writing, I don't care if the boy looks like a damn troll."

FINN'S CHRISTMAS

ENDANGERED FAE 1.5

ANGEL MARTINEZ

SILVER PUBLISHING
Published by Silver Publishing
Publisher of Erotic Romance

Dedication

To my parents, who patiently indulged my never-ending hunger for myth and folklore from a very young age. My Golden Treasury of Myths and Legends still sits on my shelf.

Finn's Christmas

"*Mi vida*? Don't you want a little something? You haven't eaten in days." Diego perched on the edge of the bed, concern knotting his stomach.

The blanket nest stirred and muttered an incoherent phrase, most likely nothing polite.

He tried again. "I brought you chicken *enchiladas*, the ones with Tia Carmen's *mole* sauce. And some hot chocolate if you don't think you can stand anything else."

"I've no appetite. Let me sleep." Finn's mumbled response drifted out from under the pillows.

"You've been sleeping since Thursday. Today's Saturday, if you happen to care, and Miriam's on her way up to visit."

"Miriam?" The grumble took on a plaintive tone.

"Yes, *corazón*, Miriam. Don't you want

to see her?" Diego stroked what he assumed was Finn's back.

The arrival of serious snow in late November had brought on this odd, increased lethargy. Finn began to eat less and less; his usual manic energy dwindled to a trickle. The decline continued until a week before the solstice. He crawled into bed and refused to come out of his circular nest of pillows and blankets.

Do pookas get the flu? Diego tried an experimental tug at the top of the blankets and sighed when Finn pulled them tighter over his head. "*Cariño*, this has to stop…"

He put the plate down on the bedside table to try a new angle of attack. One of Finn's long, elegant feet, among his most sensitive body parts, peeked out of the nest. Before he could mount a retreat, Diego flipped the covers up to Finn's knees and pulled the resisting foot into his lap. His thumb massaged the instep while his fingers caressed the ball. Long toes curled, the foot stretched and flexed, and a soft moan vibrated under the blankets.

Diego slid his hand up under the covers, over the back of one smooth, lean thigh, to stroke the perfect globes of Finn's muscular butt. "I miss you," Diego whispered. "Come out and tell me what's wrong."

A soft whimper answered, but Finn stayed stubbornly submerged. Diego slid his hand around the curve of hip, a smile tugging at his lips as Finn's cool skin shivered under his palm. He found a swiftly stiffening cock waiting for him, and his smile faded as his fingertips caressed the shaft. The chill extended even there, and though Finn's body temperature was a few degrees cooler than human by nature, he always exuded heat when excited.

Something's very wrong here. He wrapped Finn's cock in his fist and pumped slowly from base to crown until Finn unwound enough to roll on his back and spread his legs. When his hips pushed up in entreaty, Diego abruptly withdrew his hand.

The covers flew back, Finn's black eyes tinged in red as he glared at Diego. "You stopped," he whispered.

"Yes. If I bring you to climax you're sure to fall back to sleep. Get up, *mi vida*. We need to get you presentable before she gets here."

Moving as if his bones ached, Finn sat up against the headboard. His eyes immediately slid shut again.

"Finn!" Diego took him by the upper arms and shook him hard. "What the hell's wrong with you? I can't help you if you don't tell me."

"Perhaps… some of your swamp mud…" Finn mumbled, his head falling forward with a thump onto Diego's shoulder.

"You want coffee? I don't know if that's a good idea on an empty stomach."

"Miriam."

The word whispered against Diego's throat, sending a sharp frisson of need through him. Damn it, it had been over a week since they made love. "All right, I guess we better try something."

He hauled Finn up to his feet, wrapped a blanket around his long, lean frame, and half-supported, half-carried him down the stairs.

"*Dios.* I don't suppose you could shift to something smaller?" Diego asked. Six and a half feet of stumbling pooka was a lot to manage. Finn made no attempt to answer or change his form, so Diego struggled on in silence.

In the kitchen, he tried three times to prop Finn up on one of the chairs and finally gave up, letting him curl into a ball on the floor while the coffee brewed.

How strong do you make coffee for one of the fae? Diego scrubbed his hands over his face and hoped they could avoid any nasty reactions like Finn had to chlorine and certain types of glue.

Plenty of cream and sugar joined the coffee in Finn's favorite mug with the picture of Van Gogh's *Irises* on it, and Diego crouched down to shake him. Deep, even breathing told him Finn was out again.

"Damn." Diego put the coffee down, slid down onto the floor, and unwrapped the blanket from around Finn's hips. His shaft lay on his stomach, half-erect still, beautiful in its uncut perfection. Diego lowered his head and licked up the underside. Finn stirred and moaned. Gently, he took the hardening shaft into his mouth and suckled until Finn's hands gripped his hair.

Finn let out a tortured groan when he pulled back. "Sadist," he muttered, a word he had learned recently.

"No, if I were a sadist, I would have all sorts of interesting and painful toys lying around to try on you. Sit up. Drink your coffee." Diego pulled and tugged until Finn sat with his back against the cabinets.

Finn hunched over the steam, the mug nearly disappearing in his long fingers. He sipped, made a face, sipped again, and shuddered. "Dreadful."

"Okay, so coffee goes on the short list of things you'd rather not put in your stomach. Normally. Now tell me what's happening, *cariño*. What in the world is wrong with you?" Diego stroked a lock of tangled blue-black hair from his eyes.

"Winter."

"Winter?"

"Yes."

"Are you saying you always get like this during midwinter?" Diego struggled to puzzle out what he meant.

"Not… always." Finn took a long pull at the coffee and seemed better able to hold his head up. "Sometimes. A few days or weeks of sleep."

"You... hibernate?" Diego blinked. He had never considered that. "What do you... I mean, isn't it dangerous? Sleeping for weeks? What if something comes along that wants to hurt you?" He rose from the floor and padded to the microwave to reheat the *enchiladas*.

"I burrow." Finn's answer came back oddly muffled.

"You what?" Diego turned and saw only the blanket in a heap. He hooked a finger under one edge and lifted to find a large, black badger where Finn had been, the coffee mug still clutched in its claws.

"Burrow," Badger-Finn growled.

"Oh."

He folded the blanket back from the furred head and sat down beside him. "A little better?"

"Beginning to be." The black muzzle

nudged at Diego's hand. "I am sorry, my hero, that I've worried you."

"I thought you were sick." He reached out for the mug, careful of thick, digging claws. "Here, you should shift back. I don't think badgers drink coffee."

With a grunt, Badger-Finn relinquished his hold. Blue light danced over his fur and he melted into an indistinct glow, his shape elongating and reshaping until human Finn once more sat on the kitchen floor.

Diego took him under the arms and helped him into a chair. "Please eat, *querido*. Make me happy."

Finn took a tentative sniff of his lunch, and then with a pleased growl, devoured the first *enchilada* in three bites. He held out his mug for a refill without slowing down on the second one.

"Half a cup," Diego insisted.

Intent on his food, Finn didn't argue. The

caffeine in chocolate had never bothered him, but his body's reactions were unpredictable. Black tea had caused a fit of tremors once.

"Any idea what brought this all on?" Diego asked as he wiped down the counters.

"Too blasted cold here," Finn grumbled. "Winters are dark in Eire, but not so harsh."

"Ah."

Quiet settled over the kitchen as Diego cleaned and Finn ate like a ravenous wolf. Diego became so lost in his own thoughts, he jumped and yelped when a hand landed on his hip.

"Your pardon," Finn breathed against his ear. "I did not wish to startle you." He slid up against Diego's back, erection pressing against his denim-clad butt. "I'm feeling much more awake."

"I guess so," Diego whispered as those long-fingered hands stroked his chest and stomach. Finn popped the button on his fly and slid his hand under the waistband. "God... I've missed you so... missed this. Not used to being celibate anymore."

Finn turned him gently and lifted his head for a tender kiss. "My heart, my light, if you needed relief, why didn't you seek out another lover while I slept?"

Diego peeled out of his shirt, desperate to feel skin against skin, and wrapped his arms around Finn's ribs. "I know it's hard for you to understand, but I can't."

"Of course you can." Finn nibbled along his jaw and kissed a searing line down his throat. "You are beautiful and charming and—"

"And completely devoted to you. Oh, dear God." Diego let his head fall back as his knees turned to sand under Finn's sudden passionate onslaught. "I'm yours, *mi vida*, and no one else's. I can't just hop into bed with someone else."

A growl rumbled in Finn's chest as he

slid Diego's jeans and boxers down to mid-thigh. "But I don't wish for you to be lonely and in misery."

"Only you," he whispered. "I won't have anyone else."

Finn straightened, eyes searching his face. Then he seized Diego by the waist and lifted him off the floor. His astounding strength had been unnerving at first, but now Diego found it arousing, a lover who could wrestle him to the floor, but in whose hands he was completely safe.

Two steps forward and a turn later, Diego found himself bent over the kitchen table.

"Stay there, my love," Finn demanded softly with a pat to his naked backside.

Diego rolled his hips to rub his erection against the cool wood. "Yessir."

The fridge door opened and closed behind him, and he yelped when something cold and slippery touched his crease. "Holy shit—

what's that?"

Finn took his time answering, letting the substance tease over his puckered entrance before he slid the pad of one long finger inside. "It's just butter, love. Relax."

"Butter?" Diego laughed. "Are you getting me ready or basting me?" He moaned as a second finger slid inside him.

"Perhaps a bit of both," Finn whispered, and nipped his shoulder. "Would you mind if I took a nibble or two?"

"*Dios...* do whatever you want with me." Diego gasped at the invasion of a third finger, all three stroking deep inside him to caress his gland. Finn often took the initiative, but there was something demanding about his current need, his sudden dominance new and exciting.

"I'm fairly certain you know what I want," Finn murmured against his throat as he withdrew his fingers.

A moment later, Diego felt the nudge of Finn's slick head against his backdoor. He lifted his hips in invitation, expecting the usual slow, careful approach. He cried out when he was impaled in one hard thrust instead. He clawed at the table, the pain only driving his desire higher. Finn slowed, covering him, kissing his shoulder while he adjusted.

"*Cariño...* I'm so close already. Take me, please. Don't wait for me."

Finn's growl vibrated against his back and sharp teeth fastened on his shoulder as Finn began to thrust in short, forceful strokes. Each down-stroke hit unerringly against that sweet spot deep inside, and Diego squirmed with need, rubbing his cock against the oak supporting him.

"Oh, yes," he gasped out as his balls drew up in a sudden rush. "Oh, God, yes. Just like—Finn!" He lost the power of speech as his orgasm slammed up from his core, his cries echoing off the kitchen walls. Finn's joined his only a moment later, his thrusts frenzied, his sharp nails digging into Diego's hips.

For a moment, Finn lay panting against his back. "How long before Miriam arrives?" he asked as he pulled out with greater care than he had entered.

"An hour, maybe," Diego murmured, dazed and sated, the sticky remains of his pleasure threatening to glue him to the tabletop. "And since it's that time of year, she may even bring presents."

"Time of year?"

"Christmas. Yule. Solstice. Whichever you prefer for the season."

Finn heaved himself up, and a visible shudder ran through him. "I should have a shower then, I suppose, even if it's not as if she has never seen me just after waking, though you will most likely tell me this is not the same thing, so an hour should provide enough time, one would think—"

Diego stared after him as Finn wandered out of the kitchen, still chattering on in rapid-fire phrases. He shook his head. "I hope that wears off before she gets here."

* * * *

Unfortunately, by the time Miriam pulled up the long drive, it had only gotten worse. Finn still rambled on and on, apparently without stopping for breath, while he paced in agitated circles.

With a palm to his chest, Diego halted him. "Christ. Your heart's going like a jackhammer."

"It is rather rapid, I'll grant, I can feel it throbbing in my fingertips, does this often happen? With the coffee, that is? Or is it simply a matter of—"

"Shh. Hush." Diego gave him a soft kiss to stop the ceaseless flow of words. "No more coffee for you, *querido*. I liked the aphrodisiac part, but now you're scaring me."

They watched through the floor-to-ceiling front windows, Finn trembling in Diego's arms, as Miriam levered her bulk out of her SUV. Body-type labels such as 'plus-sized' were completely inadequate for her presence. He often thought of her as a human tank—the original unstoppable force—and thanked the twists of fate that she had agreed, years ago, to be his agent. More than his agent, she was his friend and his eternal champion, lending him her New Brunswick house when the city made Finn ill, and badgering him to believe in his writing when even he had given up.

"Try to calm down." He gave Finn one last hard hug before he answered the door.

Finn sucked in deep breaths, arms wrapped around his chest, his eyes huge as saucers. "Trying, trying, trying, my hero. With all I have."

"Anybody home?" Miriam called as she stomped up onto the porch.

Diego flung open the door with a bright smile. "Hey! Hope the drive up wasn't too bad. Come in, please." He laughed at himself. "Not like I should be inviting you into your own house."

Miriam let out a little snort. "Don't use it much except in the summer, anyway, kiddo." She put her bags down and caught him in a bone-crunching bear hug. "Damn, it's good to see you. And you, too, gorgeous." She turned to Finn, arms held wide. He came to embrace her, his nervous energy turning the gesture into a little impromptu waltz around the foyer before he let her go.

She laughed. "Well, that's not a hello I get a lot of." Hands on his arms, she held him back to look him up and down. "Little on the skinny side. Isn't Diego feeding you? What's the matter, pretty boy? Silver tongue not working?"

A strangled sound caught in Finn's throat, panic in his eyes. The flood of words exploded as if they had been held under pressure. "Hello, Miriam, it's so good to see you, we haven't had a visit from you since before the leaves turned and Diego said you might stay for a day or two and he said there might be presents and I've so wanted to show you some of the new paintings I've done since then, since you were here last, that is, I think I shall, what a perfectly splendid idea—"

He broke off and dashed down the hall to the back of the house, presumably to the study that he used as his artist's studio in bad weather.

Miriam blinked twice before she cleared her throat. "Hon, you know I love your gorgeous hunk of man, but what the hell's wrong with him?"

Diego ran a hand back through his hair; certain gray ones would join the black before the end of the day. "Bad coffee reaction."

"How much did you give him? A tanker truck?"

"Closer to a cup and a half."

"You're shitting me." Miriam stared at him.

"No, I'm not. He doesn't usually drink it. Can't stand the smell." Diego had never lied outright to Miriam about Finn, but he had never told her what Finn truly was. As far as she knew, he was a gorgeous artist from Ireland whom Diego had picked up at some nightspot in New York. The time just never seemed right to tell her Finn was a magical being who should have been confined to folklore. He winced at the clatter from the back of the house.

"So why now?"

"He's been having trouble staying awake this past week. Ever since the clouds rolled in—"

"Here it is!" Finn raced back in, a canvas

clutched in both hands, a manic grin on his face. "Tell me what it is, dear lady, since I know some of them are difficult for hu—ah, people to tell, but this one should be easy if you just look at—"

"Finn!" Diego shouted over him. "Take a breath."

He drew in a deep breath, his trembling telegraphing to the canvas he held.

Miriam took a step closer to view the painting. On a background of summer-sky blue stood an indistinct white figure, roughly the shape of a one-handled rolling pin. Finn had experimented with white, finding to his great delight that there were myriad *shades* of it, and the final effect was one of a glowing nimbus surrounding the central figure. He even signed the work with the ornate 'F' he had taught himself to write.

"It's beautiful, hon. It's an angel," Miriam said with confidence.

Finn's nervous laugh skittered from him. "An angel? No, it's not that, since I've never seen one to know what they look like, do they really have those absurd bulky wings sprouting from their shoulders? I don't think it's bloody likely since they'd fall over backward with the damn heavy things, just too unbalanced, no, it's Diego, the way I see him, he's so lovely and, oh! There's another one!"

He pressed the canvas into Diego's hands and dashed away to the study again.

"This better wear off soon, or he'll go into cardiac arrest," Diego muttered.

"Maybe we should get him to a doctor." Miriam's expression hovered between worry and amusement.

"He won't go. Hates doctors."

They waited, but Finn did not return, and the sounds of rummaging from the back of the house had ceased long since. "Maybe we better check on him."

Miriam agreed, and they made their way to the back of the house cautiously, in case Finn should come careening around a corner. They found him in his studio, curled in a ball on the rug, fast asleep.

"See?" Diego waved a hand in exasperation. "Like some weird form of seasonal narcolepsy."

"Hmm." Miriam rummaged in her suitcase-sized handbag. "Hardest damn caffeine crash I've ever seen. How hard will he be to wake up?"

"Very. You could shake him and yell at him... Miriam, what—? No, wait, don't—"

The air horn blared before he could stop her from pressing the button. Finn jerked into a crouch, teeth bared, eyes glazed. He snarled, sniffed the air twice, crawled the few feet to Diego to put his head on his foot, and went back to sleep.

"Shit. That's not normal," Miriam

muttered.

"No kidding." Diego fought not to roll his eyes. "Besides letting him sleep all the time, I don't know what to do with him."

"You can't let him do that, kiddo. He'll starve to death." Miriam's forehead creased in thought. "I've never seen it like this before, but I think maybe it's S.A.D."

"He's not depressed, he's sleeping."

"Not sad, S.A.D—seasonal affective disorder. Hits a lot of people up here since the days get so short. Maybe he just needs a good sunlamp."

That doesn't explain it, Finn's nocturnal. "He doesn't—" Diego stopped abruptly. Nocturnal, yes, even with the adjustments he had made to Diego's schedule, but every day possible, he took a long nap in the afternoon sun. With the sunlight reduced to five hours a day at best, and then down to nothing with all the snow, maybe it did explain the sudden need to hibernate.

"Dan's probably got them at the hardware store," Miriam offered. "I could run down there."

"Hmm? Oh, no, Miriam, you just drove umpteen hours from the city. Would you stay with him for me? I'll run down there since it looks like the snow's stopped for now."

With chains on the truck's tires, Diego had gotten good at driving in the snow, deep in spots, but nothing like the slush and black ice of New York. Dan did indeed keep the right variety of sunlamp in stock, and Diego returned only a few hours later to a quiet house. Miriam had even mustered enough maternal instinct to tuck Finn in with pillows and blankets, though he remained on the floor.

"I hope this works." Diego set up the lamp to shine directly on Finn and then sat beside him to take his head in his lap. "*Pobre amor*. Please get better."

Two hours later, Finn stirred on his own. He rolled to his back and gazed up at Diego. "Good morning, my hero. Are you saving me from myself again?"

He combed his fingers through the inky silk of Finn's waist-length hair. "I'd fight dragons for you if I had to. Though I'd rather not have to. And it's almost dinnertime."

Finn chuckled, and then cried out when he tried to sit up. "Ach, bloody, blasted head. Feels like it's full of jagged rocks."

"No more coffee for you. Ever."

"I'll mount no protest on that account."

While Diego cooked dinner, Finn sat at the kitchen table sipping willow-bark tea and talking more sensibly to Miriam. She brought presents out of her bags for both of them while they waited—a box of good sable brushes and a black silk shirt for Finn, and a pair of arctic weather gloves for Diego.

"I need you to protect your fingers,"

Miriam explained. "Gotta keep those little digits typing on your dragon edits."

They both thanked her, and Diego kissed her cheek before he went back to the stove.

"Why do people give presents in winter?" Finn rested his head on his arms.

Miriam laughed. "Because it's Christmas, silly boy."

"And if you have never celebrated Christmas?"

"Well, then, Hanukah or Solstice or Yule, or whatever. Why are you asking, sweetie? I know they've got Christmas in Ireland."

Diego rescued them before the conversation became too bizarre. "I think he means in a more general sense. People give presents for lots of reasons, *mi vida*. Sometimes to gain favor or as part of a courtship or because it's the socially accepted thing, like for a birthday. Some people only give presents because they want to get them."

"Rather mercenary."

"Yes, it is. But I think this time of year, for a long time, people have gathered closer together because it's darker and colder. You just feel warmer about your family and friends, the people you love. And the best reason to give presents is to see the light in their eyes."

"Oh."

Finn sounded so suddenly despondent; Diego whirled to look at him. "What's the matter?"

"I have nothing to give Miriam."

"Oh, hey, gorgeous, don't sweat it." Miriam gave his arm a pat. "Starving artist and all. It's not like I expect it."

When Finn was uncharacteristically silent all through dinner, Diego put it down to exhaustion and headache. Apparently, he had been deep in thought, though.

"Miriam," he said finally. "Could I give

you the painting of Diego?"

"Oh, hon, no," Miriam said with a snort. "That's an incredible piece. You need to sell that."

"I have no wish for a stranger to have it. You think it beautiful. I would like to give it to you." He turned to Diego, one black brow arched. "Am I not doing this correctly?"

Diego laced his fingers with Finn's. "Perfectly, *mi amor*. Please, Miriam, it would mean a great deal to him for you to have it. You helped us so much, been nothing but kind to us."

"Don't you ever say that where people can hear," Miriam grumbled. "*Kind*. Trying to ruin my reputation." She took Finn's free hand. "Thanks, gorgeous. It's a very thoughtful gift."

Her eyes shone with a suspiciously wet glint, and Finn managed his first brilliant smile in weeks.

* * * *

Finn lay curled under his indoor sun on the soft nest of blankets Diego had made for him in the study. He found if he lay naked, letting the light hit as much of his skin as possible, his energy increased. Clothes were such a bother in any case.

Miriam had been so pleased with his present, still beaming as she left that morning to visit family on Prince Edward Island, and her delight had wrapped a warm glow about Finn's heart. He rather liked the feeling. Giving was a new experience, a difficult one if a person had never owned anything before to give, although he supposed one could give other things as gifts—pleasure, peace, comfort. Or did those not qualify as gifts?

He buried his head under his pillow, confused all over again.

The Winter Solstice, one of the four days of the year when the tides of magic ran highest, was the next day. It struck him as the most appropriate day for the giving of gifts from everything Diego had said.

Diego, for whom he had battled a monster, for whom he would move the very stars if he could, his love, his light... yet with all his knowledge and the centuries behind him, he had no inkling of what to give him. He so wanted to see Diego's eyes shine the way Miriam's had, those eyes the color of rich, dark loam, so expressive, so often sad.

For the love of his life, and of several earlier lifetimes, a painting simply would not do. He needed to make a grand gesture, to find some way to show him how his heart sang simply thinking of Diego, his brave, kind, passionate, brilliant Diego.

He stretched cat-wise and wandered out in search of Diego, whom he found in the den watching the picture box. *The teevee*, he reminded himself. A beautiful young woman wailed over her presumably dead lover in the picture. Diego sat clutching a pillow to his chest, jaw clenched, a sure sign he fought against sorrow.

Finn flung himself onto the sofa and pulled Diego's head against his shoulder. "Why do you watch things which cause you pain, my hero?"

"I'm sorry, *cariño.*" Diego snuggled close, relinquishing the pillow to wrap his arms around Finn's ribs. "Why are you wandering around the house naked in the dead of winter?"

"I'm quite warm from being under my little sun. You—" he poked at Diego's chest "—are ducking the question."

"It's a good play, but it always gets to me. They're so young and so in love. They should have been happy."

Finn winced as the girl plunged a dagger into her breast and fell across her lover to die. *Naught but a story, only playacting.* "What causes this misery?"

While Diego related a brief account of the story, Finn struggled to understand the details. It all seemed so convoluted and unnecessary. "Why didn't she simply go away with him? If they knew they were life-mates, why this strange, secret marriage? Why marry at all? It only seems to cause anguish and strife. All the screaming."

"You've been watching *Bridezillas* again, haven't you?"

"Perhaps a bit."

Diego tipped up his face to give him a soft, tender kiss that shot lightning right down to his toes. "It's not always like that. Promises between humans are important. The promise to be faithful, the promise of forever."

"Even when they often break these promises?"

Diego let out a soft chuckle, though Finn could feel the sadness rolling from him in waves. "Even so, *corazón*. The human heart is absurdly optimistic. When you love someone, you trust them, and believe with all your heart that the promise will be kept. Which makes the story that much sadder, because those two intended to keep their promises, but fate still ripped them apart."

Finn gripped Diego tighter, an ambush of memory tightening iron bands around his chest.

'Close your eyes, Finn! Do not watch, love! They cannot force you to watch!' The roar of flames, the stench of searing flesh and oh, dear goddesses, the screams of his beloved as he burned alive...

"Finn… Finn!" Diego had his head in both hands, searching his face in a worried way.

"It's all right, my heart. I'm well enough. An old recollection, nothing more."

"You went white as frost. I thought you were fainting. The bad one?"

"Yes, love. That one."

"There are no witch hunts anymore, *querido*. I'm here with you again."

"It only took seven hundred years," Finn grumbled.

"Might not have if you hadn't gone into the Dreaming for so long."

"Your pardon, my hero. I am sorry."

Diego pushed him back until he lay flat on the couch. "You can show me how sorry you are, then."

They made love as they had not in weeks, slowly and tenderly, exploring every part of each other as if it was the first time, lingering over every sensitive point in an exquisite game of sensual torture.

When Diego, sated and exhausted, finally lay asleep with his head on Finn's chest, Finn fell back into his ruminations. He drifted in the twilight state of half sleep, bits of conversation and memory skittering over his thoughts. His eyes snapped open on a sudden revelation.

"Of course," he whispered. "I am such a great fool."

He waited until after dinner and another bout of mating, after which Diego again fell into a sound sleep. Then he slipped from their bed and out the front door, into the chill black of Midwinter's night. He stopped on the front porch to undo the little glass light container, what was it called? *Bulb.* Just in case Diego woke and came searching for him, he didn't want to reveal his efforts until morning.

The cold affected his body not a whit, clothed or not, except for the irresistible lethargy he already felt creeping in on soft feet. He would need to hurry, or risk falling asleep before he finished.

He summoned the flows of magic to his fingertips and reached for the water, his element, all around him, in the air, the ice, and the snow piled about around the house. A different sort of artwork for Diego, with a different sort of purpose. It would be temporary, but he hoped its very fragility would render it more beautiful in his eyes.

Swiftly, silently, he worked until well after midnight, expending more energy in creation than he had in centuries. With the last piece in place, he sank to his knees in the snow, satisfied but utterly exhausted.

He told himself it would be best to go inside, but his eyes refused to stay open and his feet would not obey to take him. Finn curled up in the snow bank and went to sleep.

* * * *

Diego woke with a start and stared at the clock. Two in the morning, and the other side of the bed was empty and cold. Had it been summer, he would have assumed Finn had gone out hunting in the moonlight.

This below-zero weather, though, with more snow falling, was not good hunting weather for a pooka. He rolled out of bed, threw on a robe, and padded downstairs.

"Finn! Are you down here?" No one prowled about in the kitchen looking for a pre-dawn snack, no one in the studio on a midnight inspiration, and no unable-to-sleep pooka in the den watching bad late-night TV.

The anxiety clawing at his insides evolved to an icy wash of fear when he realized the front door stood unlocked. The wind tugging at the corners of the house gave him a terrible feeling of *déjà vu*, which the failure of the porch light to turn on only worsened. Not that he thought Finn would be foolish enough to run off and waken a *second* wendigo, but there could be other fell things lurking in the woods.

He pulled on a pair of boots, took the fireplace poker and a flashlight in hand, and stepped out onto the snow-swept porch.

"Finn! Damn it, where are you?"

Only the wind answered. Clouds blanketed the moon, impossible to see beyond the rectangles of light from the front room windows.

"Damn, damn, and damn." He stepped carefully through the miniature drifts, feeling for the porch step, letting the flashlight roam over the patch of snow-covered lawn directly in front of the house. "*Dios ayudame*, what the hell is that?"

A snow-covered lump lay at the bottom of the porch steps, not a natural drift or a hump that might be caused by an ornamental stone. This was far too large and appeared to have frozen… what? Hair?

"Oh, God… Finn." Diego rushed down the steps, clumsy in his boots, and stumbled to his knees by the strange drift. Flashlight and poker lay abandoned in the snow while he dug furiously, fingers soon frozen, though he barely noticed.

"*Querido, mi vida, mi amor*, what were you doing out here?" he lamented as he uncovered enough of Finn to pull him from the snow bank. Finn's skin had an unhealthy blue tinge and, though he no longer appeared to breathe, he had an odd little smile on his face.

Fighting panic and driven by adrenaline, Diego lifted the long frame in his arms and rushed back inside, where he placed Finn on the oversized ottoman by the fireplace. He put his ear to Finn's chest. The logical part of him knew an hour or two in the snow could never kill one of the *fae*, but relief still flooded through him to hear that beloved heart still beating.

"You idiot. I'm going to be so pissed at you when you're better."

Finn lay limp and unresponsive while Diego dried him, wrestled him into flannel pajamas, and wrapped him in the electric blanket. He started a fire, fetched more blankets from upstairs, and then curled up with Finn to hold him, pressing his chilled face to his chest for good measure. He heaved a long, shuddering sigh. At least nothing worse had happened, and Finn was safe in his arms again.

* * * *

Diego jerked awake. Gray daylight filtered in through the trees, and as his back complained, he recalled why the ottoman was not the best place to fall asleep. Beside him, Finn stirred and nuzzled at his throat.

"Good morning, my hero," he said, his voice hoarse and groggy.

Diego lifted up to one elbow to glare at him. "What the hell did you think you were doing last night? Were you *trying* to turn yourself into a pookascicle?"

"Ah. You are angry with me. Please,

please don't be. Not until I've given you your present, at least."

"Present?"

"Yes, for the Solstice." Finn untangled himself from the blankets and rose, none too steady, as he staggered to the windows. He waved for Diego to join him. "Come, love, come and see."

Every cautious nerve on edge, Diego went to him, and even let Finn wrap an arm around him as he peered out. The sun chose that moment to overtop the trees, and Diego gasped in undisguised wonder.

The space between the house and the woods had transformed from yard and driveway to a fantastic sculpture garden of wondrous, ethereal shapes. Ice spheres and arches of snow, graceful spirals and spires, parapets and polyhedrons, all decorated in a frost filigree of such delicacy, a snow spider might have spun it. The ice crystals shattered the sunlight in a thousand diamonds and blinding rainbow prisms, a riot of green, blue, and gold amidst the pristine white. In the center of this hibernal wonder stood two of the one-handled rolling pin figures Finn used to represent people in his art, one taller than the other, their forms joined by a single, slender bridge of frost decorated with lunettes and gleaming parabolas.

"Finn—" Diego gaped, unable to find adequate words. "For me?"

"For you, my heart." Finn took his hands and dropped to one knee. "Only for you."

"What's this?" Diego's chuckle came out as a strangled croak. "A proposal?"

Finn's black eyes gazed up at him, as serious as Diego had ever seen him. "A promise, my promise, to you, that while you live, while you breathe, in this or any other lifetime, I am yours and yours alone. While you are with me, as long as you will have me, I will seek no other mate, no other's bed, no other's kiss but yours."

The backs of Diego's eyes stung. Finn had gone to such incredible lengths for him, had tried so hard to understand what he most needed. His heart filled to bursting with gratitude and love. He had to clear his throat twice before he could speak. "You don't have to—"

Finn laid a finger over his lips. "I know, my hero, my life, my light. This is my gift. Freely given."

"Thank you." Diego heaved a shuddering breath and managed a little smile. "It's a wonderful, amazing gift. Happy Solstice, *mi vida*."

Finn rose, searching his face. "You are no longer angry with me?"

"No, I'm not mad. Though I should be." He smacked Finn's chest in a halfhearted way. "You scared the hell out of me last night."

"Your pardon."

"S'okay, done's done. And you certainly

redeemed yourself. You want breakfast? Pancakes, maybe?"

"Are there the little chocolate bits to go in them?"

"Of course there are chocolate chips. And sausage and bacon, and those apple turnovers you like…"

"Mmm, delicious," Finn murmured as he nuzzled behind Diego's ear.

He moaned as Finn's hands slid inside the waistband of his pj's to cup his butt. Finn's lips fastened on the side of his throat, and he melted against that long, lean body.

Breakfast would just have to wait.

The End

Also by Angel Martinez:

Available from **Silver Publishing**:

Gravitational Attraction
Vassily the Beautiful

ENDANGERED FAE
Finn
Finn's Christmas
Diego

Available from **Amber Allure**:

A Different Breed
Boots
Fortune's Sharp Adversary

Available from **Romance First**:

Aftermath

Available from **Angel's Website**:

If One Dream Should Fall and Break
Hearts and Flowers: A Tale of Hay Fever and Bad Decor

Lightning Source UK Ltd.
Milton Keynes UK
UKOW051814060812

197135UK00001B/108/P

9 781614 956440